Jane Hetherington's

Adventures in Detection: 2

PANDORA'S BOX

Nina Jon

PANDORA'S BOX
Jane Hetherington's Adventures in Detection: 2

Nina Jon

Copyright © 2012 Nina Jon

Table of Contents

CHAPTER ONE
February

With the arrival of a new and intriguing enquiry in her inbox, it looked as though the second month of Jane Hetherington's new life as a private detective was going to be as busy and as interesting as the month before.

'I don't want to say too much in writing, but I need help,' the e-mail began. 'Someone is sending me anonymous letters, threatening to reveal something I did many years ago. If it gets out, my life's over (I haven't killed anyone – promise!) I need someone who can find out who's sending the letters and put a stop to it. I don't want the police involved and my husband mustn't find out. Do you think you can help?'

In her study, Jane leant back in her chair. Had anyone asked her a couple of months earlier what she thought private detective work entailed, she'd have replied – Oh, nothing more exciting than tracking down missing poodles, most likely. How wrong she'd been. A more eventful month than the previous, would be hard to imagine – or a more tragic one.

As a widow in her sixties, Jane guessed she wasn't a textbook private eye, and her decision to become one eccentric, some might say barmy. Her daughter, Adele, had been horrified at the idea.

"What if something happens to you, mum?" she'd screamed.

"I'm a shrewd enough operator not to put myself in any danger, Adele," she'd replied calmly. "It comes down to this. Your father is dead. You have your own family, your own life. I'm sixty-three years of age. I might live for another twenty years. Even another forty.

What am I to do with my time? I'm unlikely to find work at my age, even if I'm inclined to take on a job; and besides I've been born with a trait which allows me to solve the most impenetrable of mysteries. Let's face it; I've been doing it all my life. Why not make use of it and keep myself gainfully self-employed and my little grey cells exercised, that's what I say."

"Do you actually know how to wiretap, Jane?" her son-in-law Lee, had teased.

"No, Lee I don't. Nor do I have any idea how to plant a tracking device under a car; hack into private e-mails; or lay a bug. Nor do I have any intention of finding out," she'd said. "For one it's illegal, for two, it gets people into all sorts of trouble, and for three, where's the challenge?"

"Your stance might put off those who prefer their private detectives on the morally ambiguous side," Lee'd joked.

"That it might Lee, but underhand practices and modern technology can't solve every case. Sometimes only brains and old-fashioned detective work will do it. My website will say the same thing."

In her study, she smiled when she thought back to this conversation. Lee might well be right, but so far her stance hadn't seen her out of work, as her new enquiry proved.

She stared out of her study window. She only hoped she could help the e-mail's sender. There was something plaintiff about the words, yet at the same time, the writer was not obviously touting for sympathy. Jane couldn't help wondering what on earth the poor woman had done all those years ago which anyone would care about now. The possibilities were

6

endless. There was nothing for it. She'd take the case, if only to find out.

She replied: 'I do not consider myself to be a judgmental person, and I hope you will not find me to be one. I will listen to whatever it is you choose to tell me, with, I promise, a completely open mind and will do my best to help you. Before I can do that I must meet you. Please let me know when and where would be convenient for us to meet.

Jane Hetherington.'

A short exchange of e-mails followed, at the end of which both the time and venue of their first meeting was agreed.

Only the first of February and a new client already, Jane thought whilst reaching over to answer her ringing telephone.

"Jane, thank heavens you're in," the caller said.

Jane recognised the voice immediately.

"Mirabella! How lovely to hear from you!"

Mirabella Dawson-Jones, the rector of Failsham, was a larger-than-life character, both physically and through the loquacious nature of her personality. Although hers had been a controversial appointment, her parishioners, of whom Jane was one, adored her and hearing her voice on the end of the phone always picked Jane's spirits up enormously.

"Jane, my dear, I'm sorry but this is going to have to be a short telephone conversation," Mirabella said, barely pausing for breath. "I have a wedding to perform. I can't be fashionably late, can I? I mean, I'm not the bride, am I? I'm officiating! Anyway, I've just come off the phone to the Bailey sisters."

Jane knew the three Bailey sisters well. As a long-term resident of Failsham, it would be impossible not to, for the Bailey sisters were not only three of Failsham's most elderly residents, but three of its most eccentric.

"I'll admit to being somewhat harried when they called," Mirabella continued. "I only answered the phone because I thought it was the verger asking where on earth I was. You'll never guess what's happened?"

"What?" Jane said only to listen on in astonishment while Mirabella talked. "No!" was all she could say at the end of it.

"That's what I said. They really called to speak to Felix because he's on the local council," Mirabella said of her husband, "but he's in the Lake District, and I know nothing about it. I said you may be able to help them, now you're a private investigator."

"I will visit them immediately," Jane said.

"Would you, Jane? Would you? Oh my goodness, is that the time? I really must go, or I'll be defrocked!"

Call over, Jane left for the market square immediately, with but one thought on her mind – *Spinsters in Peril!*

CHAPTER TWO
Spinsters in Peril!

I

Very little changed in Failsham, that's why Jane Hetherington loved it so.

Naturally people had come and gone over the years – not least her dear husband Hugh, tragically taken from her the year before aged just sixty-four – but by and large Failsham remained the same idyllic British market town it had been when a youthful Hugh and Jane Hetherington first settled there.

The building which encapsulated the town's timelessness, the Failsham wool shop, stood in its market square. Jane arrived at it shortly after coming off the phone to Mirabella, to discover a closed sign prominently displayed on the shop's door. Jane couldn't remember the wool shop ever having closed early before. She knocked once and waited to be let in, rubbing her hands to keep warm. She looked up at the nearly white sky. Snow beckoned.

After some time, the door swung open to reveal Nellie Bailey clutching a cotton handkerchief, which she waved in Jane's face. "I can't see any of us surviving this," Nellie said, retreating into the wool shop, still waving her handkerchief in Jane's direction, and bidding Jane to follow her, which she did.

"Wars, famine, drought, disease, the depression, we've lived through it all," the old lady said with a sigh. "But Failsham Council will be the death of us all."

"You must tell me exactly what happened," Jane said.

9

"It's best Lettice explains," Nellie said, "she opened up this morning."

II

Lettice Bailey opened her wool shop's front door that morning as she or one of her sisters had done every morning for the last six decades of their lives and found a bright, crisp morning. All three sisters could remember a time when they would have found customers waiting for the shop to open, but those days were long past. Nowadays, the only people they could expect to find waiting on their doorstep were delivery men.

It was market day, and although only just nine a.m., already busy. Lettice scanned the market square, her eyes falling upon a young man attaching a sign to the lamppost outside her shop.

"Morning," he said.

"Morning," she replied, walking over to read the sign.

She didn't understand a word of it. It referred to the Town and Country Planning Act. "They're going to improve the market square," the young man explained. "Try and get a bit more trade in."

"Oh, what a good idea," Lettice said. "Things are a bit slow sometimes."

Market day always made the morning a little busier than usual, and by eleven a.m. she'd sold half a dozen balls of wool and two pairs of knitting needles. She'd just written this sale up in her ledger book, when the shop's brass bell rang announcing a customer. She looked up and saw one of her local councillors stepping into the shop, alongside a young woman she didn't recognise.

"Councillor Duigan. What a pleasant surprise," Lettice said.

"The pleasure is all mine, Miss Bailey," was the councillor's reply.

"Have you come to purchase some wool for Mrs Duigan, Councillor? We've just received a supply of the finest angora, should she wish to knit you a nice warm jumper?" Lettice asked. "February can be a very cold month."

As she spoke, she threw a concerned glance at his companion. Although young (but to eighty-nine-year-old Lettice, everybody looked young), the girl appeared worryingly short of breath. Lettice had no doubt the poor young thing had been frogmarched across town. Councillor Duigan was known to walk at an alarming pace. She wondered if the youngster was a relative of the councillor, or if there had been a change in the councillor's personal circumstances which she had not heard about. The young woman herself was so busy gazing around the shop wondering if she'd stepped back into the eighteenth century, that she didn't realise she was being scrutinised.

Her thoughts were interrupted by Councillor Duigan, saying, "allow me to introduce you to Sarah. Sarah is a social worker who specialises in the care and well-being of the elderly." Sarah smiled weakly.

Councillor Duigan's words immediately made Lettice suspicious. She looked at Sarah and back to her local councillor – a middle-aged man with shoulder-length grey hair, who wore bright blue spectacles, permanently held together by a pink sticking plaster after its nose ridge snapped many years earlier. If he ever wore anything other than his hunting jacket, with leather patches at its elbows, she had never seen it. Lettice always thought the councillor rather ridiculous.

"Sarah and I would like a few minutes of your and your sisters' time, if you could spare it, Miss Bailey?" he continued.

"But who will run the shop?"

"Couldn't you just close it for half an hour or so?" Sarah said.

Lettice stared at her coolly for some minutes, before replying crisply, "Young lady, this is not an emporium prone to early closing. We didn't even close early during the war, and you have no idea how difficult it was to get wool then."

"We won't take up much of your time," Councillor Duigan said.

"I'll need to consult with my sisters," Lettice said crossly, turning on her heels and disappearing through a door, which led to the rear of the property.

Alone in the shop, the councillor turned to Sarah and winked knowingly. "Told you," he said.

Sarah took this to be a reference to his earlier description of the sisters as, 'complete eccentrics. Madder than a box of toads!'

Coming from the councillor, Sarah found the comment ironic. While she waited for Lettice to reappear, Sarah studied her notes. At eighty-nine, Lettice was the eldest of the three Bailey sisters. Dotty was the middle one of the three, at eighty-seven years, and Nellie was the youngest being only eighty-two years of age. The sisters had all been born in the tiny suite of rooms above the shop, then run by their parents, and had lived in this building for the whole of their lives. None had ever married.

She glanced around the shop again. Ceiling-high dark mahogany cubicles filled with pyramids of wool, lined the shop's walls. Gilded glass mirrors, reflecting back the kaleidoscope of colours, broke up the dark wooden interior. A rail ran around the ceiling from which hung a mahogany ladder. Material, laces, ribbons and threads filled shelves behind a solid mahogany counter running along the entire length of one wall. The shop's till looked as though it came out of a museum, and the sisters still seemed to write their sales up by hand in an old-fashioned ledger book. She'd been told the shop hadn't changed since the sisters' parents day, but she was beginning to wonder whether it had actually changed since their grandparents day. Indeed some of the materials stacked high behind the counter looked as though they'd been there since then. How three old ladies managed to lift such heavy rolls down from such a height, Sarah couldn't begin to imagine.

"You'd better come through. My sisters are waiting for you in the parlour," Lettice said irritably through the connecting door. "I only hope our customers don't think we've decided to close down permanently."

In the parlour, Lettice joined her sisters on a tatty Chesterfield, while their visitors sat opposite them. The sisters held hands. Sarah looked around the seldom-used room. Ornaments collected over the years were jam-packed into French corner cabinets. Material, once deep red, but now threadbare and pale, covered the Victorian furniture. Patches were visible on the room's embossed wallpaper, the rug under her feet, and the carpet it covered. Light streamed through holes in the lace curtains, despite attempts at repair. The sisters couldn't open the windows anymore, even if the windows were capable of being opened, and the unventilated room smelt musty. To the sisters credit, there was very little dust.

The councillor began by explaining why he and Sarah were there. "You've all known me since I was a boy, so naturally I didn't want you to hear about the proposals we have for the mmrket square from the council's lawyers. I wanted to speak to you face-to-face about it…"

Lettice interrupted him. "Oh, we know all about that. I read the notice on the lamppost outside the shop. You want to improve the market square. Well, I certainly hope you're going to do something about the empty properties on either side of us."

"It doesn't help our trade one bit, those two ramshackle properties left to rot," her sister Dotty pointed out.

"We have written to you on the subject," said the last of the three sisters, Nellie.

"I know you have," Councillor Duigan said. "Our proposals will include those properties and also the wool shop. You'll receive a formal letter from our planning department in the next day or two, setting out exactly what we are intending to do, as well as your options which will include the right to make objections should you wish to. More notices will appear about town and in the papers. It's all very formal, I'm afraid. But let me tell you what we are proposing to do. The Council think it's in the best interests of the town that part of the market square is redeveloped. The other side of square, where the lovely old Georgian manor houses

14

are, will remain untouched, but your side of the market square will be included in the redevelopment. There are various stages we need to go through. There may have to be a public enquiry, although I doubt it. You'll receive a letter from us, as I have said, and should you wish to, there'll be plenty of time for you to put your point of view forward. But I have to say, the council are confident that the proposal will be passed, and the market square redeveloped for the benefit of the town and surrounding area. This brings us to Sarah. Sarah's going to help you find somewhere else to live."

The sisters glanced at each other. "We'd rather stay here when the redevelopment is going on" Nellie said.

"It'll take more than a little dust and disruption to drive us out," Dotty said.

Now it was the turn of the councillor and Sarah to glance at each other.

"I'm afraid that won't be possible," the councillor said.

"Why ever not?" Lettice asked.

"Because our plans involve demolishing this entire side of the square," Duigan said bluntly.

"You want to knock our home down?" Dotty shrieked.

"We shan't go," Lettice said.

"If the proposals go through, you won't have any choice, I'm afraid. If necessary we can compulsorily purchase the property," the councillor explained.

"You can do what you want, my boy, but you can't pull our house down with us still in it," Nellie quite rightly pointed out. She got to her feet, impressively quickly Sarah thought, and opened the parlour door. "If you want to demolish our wool shop, you'll be doing so over our dead bodies. Now I'm afraid, I must ask you to leave our property immediately, Mr Councillor Duigan, and you can take your lady social worker, Ms Sarah, with you, as we shan't be needing her services."

Nellie Bailey folded her arms, and waited for the two to leave. Her sisters moved to stand on either side of her.

"Before you make your minds up, please spend a few minutes looking at the details of the lovely homes, Sarah has bought with her," the councillor said.

Sarah produced some glossy brochures from her bag, which she held out to the sisters. "There really are some lovely old people's homes," Sarah said.

Her suggestion, or maybe her patronising tone, was the final straw for the sisters.

"Nellie, please pass me the fly squat," Dotty said to her sister.

Nellie passed the wicker fly squat – almost as tall as the sisters – to Dotty who, holding it with both hands, bought it up over her head and down on to the armchair, where the councillor would still have been sitting, had he not leapt up and run behind the armchair, seconds earlier. Sarah hastily moved to his side.

"Drat," Dotty said. "Missed. Never mind. Try, try and try again, as they say." She raised the fly squat above her head again, and attempted to hit both Councillor Duigan and Sarah with it. They hurriedly crossed the parlour room, while Dotty took another swipe at them.

Sarah threw the brochures down on the floor with the words, "Why don't we just leave them here for you to look at?"

16

She tumbled out of the door, quickly followed by the councillor, and chased after by the three old ladies.

Councillor Duigan and Sarah ran out of the shop, and into the market square, where Sarah doubled over with a stitch.

"Did I hear one of them say they still had some DDT under the stairs?" Sarah gasped.

While they struggled to get their breath back, the property brochures landed at their feet and the front door slammed shut.

CHAPTER THREE
The Failsham Wool Shop

Jane had known that whichever Bailey sister opened the door to her, the sister concerned would be dressed in a faded floral dress under a pinafore, that her stockings would be thick, her shoes flat lace-ups, and her completely white hair worn in a bun. Jane had rarely seen the sisters dressed in anything else in all the years she'd known them. As far as she could tell they hadn't replaced their clothes since the 1950s, which in her mind made their clothes more modern than their kitchen. As she'd said to Hugh many a time, "It can't have been refurbished since the property was built. Heaven only knows how they manage!"

All but transported from the Edwardian era, the sisters' kitchen was a strange looking room. Thick yellow gloss covered both its tiled walls and its wooden cupboards, in which all kitchenware was painstakingly put away by the sisters at the end of the day, even though there wasn't a piece in the place which wasn't chipped, cracked, bent, broken or missing a handle or a lid. Although the sisters promised they used the twin-tub and electric oven given to them many years earlier by a kindly neighbour, Jane wasn't convinced they actually did. The suspicion she'd long harboured that they still washed their clothes on the wooden scrubbing board which hung on the wall, and still cooked on the kitchen's original black lead, wood-fuelled stove, in situ under an old-fashioned tiled surround, was all but confirmed when she'd surreptitiously opened the stove one day, and found a chicken all ready to cook inside.

The sisters did possess a fridge but nothing as modern as a freezer or a microwave. The water heater fitted above the kitchen's original Belfast stone sink, remained the kitchen's only source of hot water.

As usual a flowery plastic tablecloth covered the kitchen table, on which stood a pot of tea and half a fruit cake. On one side of the table, the three old ladies held hands, their eyes red from crying, whilst on the other side, Jane studied them. She genuinely didn't think any of them had ever been further than the coast their whole lives and even then only on a day trip, and now they are being asked to leave their home.

"We were making plans for Lettice's ninetieth birthday, it's this summer, you know," Dotty told her, "and now we don't know where any of us will be."

Was Lettice really about to turn ninety, thought Jane. She could still remember the old lady celebrating her seventy-fifth birthday with tea in the garden, and said so, "Ninety? Goodness. I still remember your seventy-fifth, Lettice, as though it were yesterday. It was such a beautiful day we all sat out in the garden. There wasn't a cloud in the sky."

"I remember," Lettice said. "You gave me a book as a birthday present. I did so enjoy reading it. What was it called now? Oh yes, I remember – *Spinsters in Peril!* I ended up reading the whole series, I enjoyed it so much."

Jane smiled. The choice of the novel had been her late husband's. He'd gone to his grave convinced the eccentric old ladies routine no more than a clever ruse, concealing the sisters real identity as undercover sleuths: "Like in the Spinster Sister Sleuth Series," he'd always say.

"We made a pact long ago that the last of us to leave here would do so feet first," Dotty announced and on either side of her, her sisters nodded in agreement.

"We won't allow the council to knock the wool shop down," Lettice said, stamping her tiny foot as she said this.

"We shan't have it," Nellie said. "We look after what is ours, and the shop is ours."

"No, I don't suppose you shall," Jane replied, wondering whether anyone on the council had even considered they might actually have a fight on their hands over this one, and they would, they could be sure of that.

There was little else she could do at this stage, but advise them to take legal advice on their grounds for objecting to the redevelopment, and this is what she told them. As she spoke, she thought them rather disappointed in this. Something confirmed when Dotty said, "We were hoping for something more than that, Mrs Hetherington."

"Such as?" Jane asked.

"Well as you're a private investigator..." Nellie said.

"... We thought you could find something out about the council that we could blackmail them with," Dotty said.

"Blackmail?" Jane said.

"To make them back down," Lettice said.

"We appreciate it might take you time to find something, with just about anything going nowadays and no one embarrassed by anything they do," Dotty said, seemingly seriously.

"But we just haven't got enough money to bribe the whole council," Nellie said.

"That's why we've determined upon blackmail," Lettice felt the need to explain.

"Blackmail's illegal," Jane said hurriedly, "as is bribery. There are also the practicalities to consider. We'd have to unearth something against everyone on the council, most of whom you know far more about than I ever will. Even if we did, they'd probably only resign, forcing a by-election, putting us back to square one. Let's rule out blackmail or bribery. Tell you what, you make an appointment with your family lawyer, and I'll have a ponder and see what else I can come up with?" Jane got to her feet.

"If necessary we'll lock ourselves in the cellar," Dotty said.

Jane glanced towards the door to the cellar. She'd never seen inside the building's cellar and dreaded to think how steep its stairs were. Was there even a light down there which still worked, she wondered.

"We must buy in meats we can preserve for the siege," Nellie said, on the front doorstep.

"And I'll make jams and pickles," Lettice said.

"We can buy some hens and a goat for milk," Dotty said. "Then we'll need for nothing."

Jane imagined their sisters huddled around a candle in their dark, dank cellar, surrounded by jars and cans, cold meats hanging from the ceiling, chickens running around their feet and a goat chomping something in the corner. Good Lord, she thought, shaking her head at the image. She turned to say something but realised the sisters were lost in their own world, and she quietly slipped away.

Out in the market square the promised snow was falling. Jane watched a bus pull up at the bus stop and a group of youngsters got off it, led by a teenage girl. Whilst her friends danced and swirled in the thick white haze, their hands outstretched to catch the snowflakes, the girl, the smallest of the group, brushed snow away from the stone body of the white lion guarding the White Lion Hotel.

This scene reminded Jane of the winter she'd been pregnant with Adele. Failsham had been snowed in. She and Hugh were meant to attend a wedding, but the weather made driving impossible and they'd ended up donning Wellington boots, wrapping a blanket around themselves and walking to the market square to await a tractor kindly laid on by the bride's father (a farmer) to transport them to the wedding. Jane could still remember the exhilaration she'd felt marching arm in arm with Hugh through the falling snow, and her joy upon finding the square, its old dark red, Georgian townhouses, and its Christmas tree complete with twinkling lights, covered in snow.

"All we need now is for the coach and horses to appear and we'll have a Dickensian Christmas card," Hugh had said, at the precise moment the tractor emerged through the still falling snow, pulling the cart which was to carry them to the wedding. A young collie dog excitedly ran at its side, barking. The young couple could do nothing else but laugh.

Remembering this brought a lump to her throat. Was everything in Failsham about to change, she thought. She hoped not. She looked down at the home-baked rhubarb and plum pie, made with home-grown fruits, which Nellie had insisted in thrusting into her hands minutes earlier. If she didn't get it home quickly, it would be frozen solid. She turned for home.

CHAPTER FOUR
Pandora's Box

At just after ten o'clock the following morning, Jane reached the café on a quiet London side street a few blocks away from Camden market, where she'd arranged to meet her new client. She arrived at the café just as a woman with a weatherworn face, sitting alone at one of two outside tables and dressed in a trench coat and a headscarf, stubbed out a cigarette and lit another.

Even though the day was cloudy and overcast, the woman wore sunglasses. She'd even turned her collar up, as though she was the private detective waiting for a client rather than a client waiting to meet a private detective. This woman did not want to be recognized, Jane realised. She approached her.

"Roz?"

The woman got to her feet and they shook hands. A young woman appeared from inside the café to take Jane's order. A black coffee quickly appeared. As soon as it was placed on the table, the young waitress retreated back inside the café to watch television. This left Jane and Roz alone to talk.

"I chose here because the staff mind their own business," Roz said, inhaling a cigarette.

Jane couldn't immediately place the accent. It wasn't London for sure. Roz offered her a cigarette. She declined. "I gave up when I was pregnant with my daughter. Not a day has gone by since, when I haven't wanted a cigarette, but I've always resisted the temptation."

"How old is your daughter?"

"Nearly thirty-seven."

Roz laughed out loud. "I think I'd have succumbed."

"Please tell me about the letters."

"So's you'll understand what's going on, I need to go back to when I was a nipper," Roz said, her words punctuated by draws on her cigarette. She inhaled deep into her lungs, only exhaling it while she spoke. "I was always close to my dad, closer than I ever was to my mum. All she ever did was shout at us. When I was eleven, he died of a heart attack without warning. He hadn't even been ill. No one ever really talked about it. Mum completely fell apart. She started drinking. Whenever I tried to talk about what had happened, my mum would say, 'He's dead and you're going to have to live with it. Think I'm happy about it? Do you?' then she'd start shouting again or crying. I felt like a freak at school. I had a dead dad and a drunk mum. I started bunking off. Things got worse at home. Mum started drinking more. My brother and I played up. Mum couldn't cope. More than once, she drank herself unconscious. The house was worse than a pigsty. Our clothes never got washed. Sometimes we had to steal food just to get a meal. Someone must have called social services 'cause both of us were put into care. It was meant to help, but for me, it just made things worse. From then on in, I was finished. It wasn't long till the other kids had me sniffing glue and getting pie-eyed on cheap cider. By thirteen, I'd dropped out of school. Someone got me snorting heroin. They said it was a cheaper way of blocking things out than the booze. And it was. I needed a lot less of it to get into such a state I couldn't remember anything and didn't care if I did or not. It wasn't long before I was injecting.

25

When boys need money for drugs, they rob someone or break into a house. But I was a girl. I sold my body. By fifteen, I was a junkie and streetwalker. I can't tell you how much I hated what I was. I tried to tell myself I could put up with people swearing at me out of car windows, spitting as they drove past or throwing rubbish or dog shit at me, but I couldn't really. I can't tell you how bad it made me feel. I used to shout back at them, 'You pay my kid's school fees and I'll give up the game.' I wanted them to think I was more than some washed-up junkie – a waste of space. God knows why. Pathetic really. Someone even told me I was going to burn in hell – like I cared. I wasn't worried about hell. I was worried about surviving the night. However much you pretend to yourself it's going to be okay, you never know. Prostitution is a dirty and dangerous game. Once I was beaten up so bad they thought I was going to die. I don't know how I didn't. Wasn't meant to be, I guess. I tried to give the drugs up, but I couldn't. I tried methadone. Didn't work. I went back on drugs and back on the streets so many times, I lost count. I learnt to cut off. I had to. The alternative was life with no drugs and I couldn't face that. You don't know what grip the drugs have on you, until they've got you. I knew girls from good homes, with kiddies, jobs, throw it all away 'cos of the drugs. You end up not washing or eating or feeding your own kids. I've seen girls flog their kids' nappies for drugs. For years, my life was spent on the back seat of punters' cars, earning enough money for one more shot. I had a criminal record as long as my right arm and I don't know how many abortions. It's amazing I ever went on to have a kid. One day I woke up in hospital. I'd been found unconscious in a toilet cubicle, a needle by my side. 'You don't know how lucky you are to be alive,' the young medic told me. 'Don't care if I'm alive or dead, love,' I said. 'You're only twenty-six. You'll be lucky if you live to see forty if you don't stop doing this to your body, and believe me, by then, no one is going to care much,' she said. Maybe she was trying to use some sort of shock-therapy on me? Shame me into giving up the drugs. It didn't work. No sooner was I out, then I was back to my old tricks. Then something happened. One of the girls disappeared one night. A mate of mine. No one knew what happened to her. She was last seen getting in a blue car, then nothing. Her body was found months later in a river. Far as I know, no one's ever been charged. The medic was right. I wasn't going to make forty if I didn't stop. I could be the one he got next, and no one but me would care. That's what did it.

"I stopped the drugs there and then. No more shooting up. Months after I'd stopped, the urge to start again was as strong as ever. I was still getting the sweats, still shaking, still had runs, still couldn't sleep. It was as bad as when I first stopped. I couldn't do anything but walk round and round my flat for hour after hour. If it hadn't have been for my brother bringing me food, sitting up with me night after night, I wouldn't be here now. I'd be another dead junkie. But somehow I did it. I kicked the habit. I got my life back on track. That was thirty-seven years ago, Jane."

Now Jane finally knew what Roz had done all those years ago, her only thought on the subject was – is that all?

"I'm so sorry all that happened to you," Jane said, "and I'm glad you've been able to move on."

"I did move on," Roz said. "I moved on, changed my name, got married, and had a son. I'm a granny now. The past is the past. I never think about it. I block it out. My hubby and son don't know anything about it and never will far as I'm concerned. But now I've started to get these..." Roz said, putting her smouldering cigarette in the ashtray, and taking some pale blue envelopes out of her handbag, which she handed to Jane. "They're in the order I got them. I started to get them as soon as I announced I was running as a local councillor."

Jane removed the first letter from its envelope. The paper inside matched the pale blue envelope. She read the letter.

'You're not fit to run for office. There's only one word for a woman like you. I won't stoop so low as to use it, but we both know what it is!'

Home computers have certainly improved the quality of hate mail, Jane thought to herself as she read through it. Long gone were the days when the composer of such letters would have to sit at home glueing words and letters cut from newspapers onto cheap writing paper. Now it seemed hate mail was typed up in New Courier, spell checked, margined right and left, and printed out on quite high-quality paper. Jane didn't finish the letter. She folded it up and returned it to its envelope. The second letter was along the same lines.

'Women like you are not fit to breathe the same air as the rest of us, let alone run for political office. Do you think the public will forgive you your many transgressions, once they learn of them? If so, I fear

you are mistaken. Does your own husband know?
Would he have married you if he did? I doubt it.'

The third letter was even worse.

'*The good Lord and I know all about your filthy*
godforsaken ways and if you continue with your
campaign, I will ensure the whole community does too!'

This letter ended with a number of pejorative
words about prostitution and prostitutes, which Jane
declined to read. This last letter she also returned to its
envelope. Roz looked at Jane expectantly.

"What an overreaction about something which
happened over thirty years ago," Jane said.

"There are more than just those." Roz stubbed out
a cigarette, and opened a second packet, discarding its
cellophane wrapper in the ashtray along with the
crunched up empty packet. "When I got the first one, I
thought it was some kind of joke and ignored it. But
then others came. Luckily, my hubby leaves for work
before the post comes. Dunno what I'd tell him, if he
read one of these. I have to keep them in my handbag
the whole time, to make sure he doesn't see them."

"You have no idea who's sending these to you, I
suppose?"

"None. It's so long ago. I can't think who'd
remember me from back then, I'm so different now. It's
not as if it's even the same area, for God's sake."

"When exactly did these letters begin to arrive?"

"Couple of days after my photo appeared in the
paper announcing my candidacy. I didn't realise
running for the local council would open up such a
Pandora's Box."

"Someone must have recognized your photograph. Someone with a good eye for details and a good memory."

"Maybe one of the coppers who nicked me, or one of my regular punters from back then," Roz said.

"Where exactly was back then?" Jane asked.

"Greater Flyborough."

"Really? That's just down the road from where I live believe it or not. I presume you've decided against dropping out of the election to see if that makes the letters stop?"

"Why should I?" Roz said, indignantly, her eyes blazing. "I want to know who he is. We both know it's a man, let's face it."

Although she knew from statistics that women were just as likely as men to pen malicious letters, on balance, Jane agreed with Roz on this one. There was something about the letters which made her think they had most likely been sent by a man, but on the issue of the gender of the letter writer, as with everything else, she must keep an open mind.

"I want you to find the sanctimonious little git, so I can look him in the eye and ask him who the hell he thinks he is for condemning me for something he can't begin to understand."

"I admire your attitude, Roz," Jane said. "I'll do everything I can to help you. I believe the key to discovering the sender of these letters lies in the present, not in the past. Tell me all about the life you live now, and a little bit about the place where you now live, if you don't mind. But first, let's order some more coffee."

The ladies talked on for more than an hour, before parting company.

On the coach home, Jane took a window seat and stared out the window, thinking about Roz. Jane's own childhood had been, on the whole, a sheltered and happy one. Roz and she must be quite close in age, she realised, but when she'd been keeping a scrapbook, Roz had been sniffing glue. That Roz had become a drug addict and prostitute may have been inevitable, but that she was now being persecuted for something that had hurt no one but herself, wasn't. It was vindictive and spiteful, which made Jane all the more determined to unmask the culprit, and put a stop to it.

Jane glanced behind her. The seat was empty. She tilted her seat back, closed her eyes and fell asleep.

CHAPTER FIVE
The Rectory

I

The next morning, two handwritten letters arrived in the day's post, both addressed to Mrs Jane Hetherington, The Pink Cottage, Failsham, Hoven HN 14. She didn't recognize the handwriting on either of them.

The first contained an invitation to an exhibition of photographs taken by an up and coming photographer (as the invitation put it) at the Beech Hill Art Gallery, in the nearby Cathedral city of Southstoft. Jane thought the invitation, printed on stiff card, with rounded edges embossed with gold and inlaid with gold italic letters, rather formal for a photographic exhibition. She didn't know the gallery, nor the photographer whose work was being exhibited there – Mandy Tomas – nor the art dealer arranging the exhibition, Graham Burslem. Whilst she found the gallery in the *Yellow Pages,* the only Graham Burslem she could find was a local art dealer with a gallery in the coastal resort of Sailles, whom she took to be the same person. Mandy Tomas wasn't listed at all.

She couldn't help wondering from which database her name had been obtained. On the reverse of the card, below a map showing the location of the gallery, Graham Burslem had hand written,

'I do so hope you can attend. It would be such a delight if you could.

Graham Burslem'

Jane thought his words rather ebullient, and probably written on the back of every invitation he'd sent out. She read the invitation again. The exhibition was in the evening. It would mean a drive to Southstoft, but it was only twenty-five minutes away and she'd be driving against the traffic. If the invitation was to be trusted, the event would be over by eight o'clock in the evening. She'd go.

The second item of post contained a brief handwritten notelet.

'Mrs Hetherington,

I wish to engage your services. Please could you visit me? I teach Sunday school and would be pleased if we could meet there. I attach details.

Orla Wilson (Mrs)'

Attached to the note, was an information sheet giving the dates of the next ten Sunday schools and the address of the church hall where they were held.

There wasn't even a forwarding address. Orla's letter gave Jane no idea what it was she was being asked to investigate.

While Hugh hadn't been a rich man, he'd left her comfortably off. She had a good pension, unlike so many unfortunates, she owned a lovely home and had enough money in the bank to run a car, visit her daughter and son-in-law in the United States now and then, and pay for any help she needed in the home and garden. All in all she was lucky. She didn't rely on the detective agency to keep the rain off her head, and therefore could pick and choose which instructions she'd take. She'd turned down a request from a man who had wanted her to spy on his three girlfriends, in case any of them were being unfaithful to him; and from the owners of a family-run business, who'd wanted Jane to find out what their staff were up to in their spare time. She'd turned down both instructions because she hadn't liked the clients nor what they wished her to do. They'd come across as unpleasant people, and she'd wanted to have nothing to do with them.

Whilst she would have preferred to have known more about why Orla wished to engage her services, Jane understood that some of her clients had very good reason for needing secrecy, Roz, for example. The sender of this note may well have similarly good reasons for her lack of candour. Orla might be a frightened woman, with nowhere else to turn but a private detective. She would take Orla Wilson up on her invitation and visit her this Sunday. When she'd met her, then she would decide whether or not to take the case on.

II

The church where Hugh was buried was just a short walk from Jane's cottage and adjourned the rectory where Mirabella and Felix lived. Having Hugh buried so near allowed Jane to visit him whenever she wanted to, and she did so that morning. She spent some time at his graveside, laying a bunch of white and purple waterfall pansies on it, and telling him of her day thus far. When it was time for her to go, she kissed her hand and laid it on his gravestone. From the churchyard she made her way to the rectory for lunch.

After her own pink thatched cottage, the rectory was Jane's favourite property in Failsham. It was a relatively new building, having been built in the 1930s after its predecessor burnt down. Commissioned by a well-known eccentric, it came complete with a pepper pot turret, five spiral chimney stacks and numerous diamond crossed windows, of different shapes and sizes. The property had reminded Hugh of Munster Towers, and whenever they'd approached it, he'd insisted on humming the Munster's theme tune and clicking his fingers at the end of the chord. Jane however, loved the property. It was straight from a Gothic novel. She knew it to be something of a disappointment to Felix Dawson-Jones that no grisly unsolved murders had ever been committed there, causing him to joke that maybe they should commit one?

Mirabella met Jane at the door effusively and showed her into the rectory's pretty drawing room, where Felix poured her a large gin and tonic. Drink in hand, she settled down by the roaring wood fire to gaze out on the rectory's snow-covered garden through the room's French windows. Felix meanwhile, walked over to stand by the fire, drink in hand.

"I really don't think you're going to be able to persuade the Bailey sisters to sell up, Felix," Jane said. "They're determined to stay put. To be honest, I know exactly how they feel. People are always telling me the Pink Cottage is far too large for an elderly widow, and suggesting I sell it to them. But as I've said many a time, I'll sell up when I'm good and ready and not before."

"That clot Duigan most likely put his foot in his mouth again," Felix said. "It was a bit unorthodox him going to see them, but we all like the old biddies, and no one wanted them to learn of our plans from a letter. He meant well, but let's face it, he has a blunt way of putting things. I'm sure they can be persuaded to go quietly."

"I'm not so sure, Felix," Jane said. "I really think you've got a fight on your hands over this one."

"Mirabella and I will go and see them tomorrow and gently explain how much better it would be for them to swap their drafty old home for a nice double-glazed bungalow. We'll see what the old Dawson-Jones charm does," he said.

Mirabella peered imperiously at him: . "What do you mean Mirabella and I? I'm not helping you persuade three dear old ladies to leave the very house they were born in, so you can avoid unpleasantness."

"It's for their own good," Felix said, with as much authority as he could manage. "That wool shop of theirs can't earn them any money. The house is falling down around them, they can barely afford to heat it, let alone maintain it. They only live in a few rooms as it is. If they get any more infirm, they won't be able to live there at all."

"Do you remember that flat we lived in just after we married? You were still sorting out your divorce, and I was still training. It was tiny and freezing cold. It had no hot water for days on end, it was damp, and the landlord wouldn't even allow us to use an electric fire because it was too expensive. People thought we were mad to stay there for as long as we did, but we loved it because it was our first home."

"I think you may be looking back on things through rose-tinted spectacles, my sweet. We stayed there because we couldn't afford to live anywhere else. Neither of us would ever wish to live there again. Not to mention we're not touching ninety. The Bailey sisters won't want to return to that wool shop of theirs again once they've lived somewhere else."

"A few more mod cons, is all that place needs. They're not going to live forever. Either one of them will die, or their health will deteriorate to such an extent that they will have to move out anyway. Couldn't the redevelopment wait a few years?" Mirabella said.

"The market needs redevelopment now. Trade is declining. More and more people are driving out of town to do their shopping. We have a developer interested in building a row of modern shop units where the wool shop is. We can fit twice as many units in there, as are there at present. It would transform the square. The ladies can put their wool shop in there if they want to," he said, clearly beginning to feel very beleaguered.

"They wouldn't earn enough money to pay the rent, Felix and you know it," Jane said gently.

"Well, they can't stay where they are," he said. "The council is committed to this."

"Isn't the building too old to knock down? Isn't it protected?" Jane enquired.

Felix shook his head. "It's old certainly, maybe Victorian, but not old enough or special enough to make it worth preserving."

"Will you physically carry them out, Felix?" Mirabella asked. "They're regular members of my congregation. We've eaten Sunday lunch at their house, and they at ours."

"It won't come to that. As I keep saying, I'm sure they can be persuaded to move. After lunch, I'll go straight round to the wool shop to a speak to them myself. If I'd gone originally instead of Duigan, all of this could have been avoided." He moved to top up the drinks with the words, "I remain confident of a constructive result."

CHAPTER SIX
Spinsters on the Warpath!

Felix's confidence in his powers of persuasion grew stronger as he walked towards the wool shop, but evaporated the instant Nellie Bailey opened the door to him, saw him standing there, and shrieked, "Lettice! Dotty! Felix Dawson-Jones has come for our home!"

"No I haven't," he tried to explain, but his words were in vain.

Dotty hurried to her sister's side. Clearly infuriated by Felix's presence on their doorstep, the two sisters stood side-by-side, their arms folded across their chests, blocking the doorway. "You're not taking our home, Felix Dawson-Jones," Nellie said to him, waving her tiny fist under his chin, something she had to stand on her tip toes to achieve.

"We'll give you good money for it – you can get somewhere much nicer. If you'll allow me in, I can show you some pictures of some lovely places where you could live."

"We live here," Dotty said. Neither she nor her sister moved an inch. His continued presence didn't seem to be doing anything other than annoying and galvanising them further.

"Here let me show you," he said, squatting down to open his briefcase. "I don't suppose I could step inside?"

"You suppose right, Felix Dawson-Jones," Nellie said, rather terrifyingly for a frail, diminutive woman in her late eighties, he thought.

Felix pulled out some of the shiny new brochures from his briefcase, only to hear something above him.

He looked up to discover the minute Lettice leaning out of one of the upstairs windows, holding a heavy jug she'd balanced on the windowsill.

"If you don't leave our premises I'll pour this jug of water over your head, I swear I will," she said.

Felix backed away, his hands in the air. He was more concerned about the jug hitting him on the head than its contents. A full jug of water was probably heavier than Lettice.

"My dear Lett …" he stopped himself. Was it Lettice, he wondered, or was that the one on the right? Or was that Nellie? Or Dotty? He suddenly realised he couldn't be sure who was who. In fact, he couldn't actually tell the sisters apart. He wondered if he'd ever actually been able to. Had he been calling each by the wrong name, all these years?

"My dear, Miss Bailey," he said. "Please see reason."

His words fell on deaf ears. The front door shut in his face.

"And your wife such a lovely woman too! You don't deserve her!" Dotty shouted through the letterbox.

No sooner had she finished her tirade, than water cascaded from the jug. Felix jumped out of the way. He looked up to see the window slam shut, and down to the ground to see a pool of water running towards his feet.

Felix moved to the middle of the square and looked back at the shop. His belief that a constructive result could easily be achieved had clearly been misplaced. From now on in, he realised bitterly, the ladies and the council were mired in the bureaucracy that was a disputed planning application – in other words, they were at war.

CHAPTER SEVEN
The Search for the Poison Pen Pal

Roz lived in a town called Marlowe-on-the-Water. She'd made the small town her home many years earlier, thinking, that there, she could safely disappear into the bustle of small-town life, her past airbrushed away forever. Jane could see why. While Greater Flyborough was a large, frenetic, transient port town, Marlowe-on-the Water was a quiet, fairly affluent town, whose residents settled for life. How uncanny for two unconnected people from Greater Flyborough to settle in Marlowe, Jane thought, but they had.

When Jane arrived in Marlowe, few were about. The letter writer persecuting Roz clearly considered himself (Jane, like Roz, had a hunch the writer was a man) to be doing the Lord's work and Jane decided to start with a visit to the town's local churches. Two churches served the parish of Marlowe on the Water – the Church of St. Martins and the Church of St. Magdalene. Jane went first to the closer of the two, the church of St. Martins.

The unassuming eighteenth century church overlooked a river. A footpath, cut through untended graves, led to its front door, and a circular tower stood at its west end. Jane pushed open its large wooden door, stepped inside and found herself alone in the small church. Biblical tapestries hung on its whitewashed walls. Arched stone frames surrounded unadorned aisle windows. Wooden pews, with hymn books laid out, lined the nave.

She walked its length and back again, her footsteps caught in the silence. Once back at the door, she picked up a copy of the Parish News, and put it into her hand bag, hoping it might contain a name leading her to the letter writer. She stopped to study the announcements covering the notice board: the dates of services, flower rosters, details of jumble sales, Bible reading classes, knitting groups, fetes and afternoons devoted to contemplative prayer. Jane read each notice carefully, but none bore any similarity, in any way, to the letters received by poor Roz. Nevertheless, she made a note of any names, including the names of the churchwarden and ladies on the flower roster.

A short walk took her to St. Magdalenes. The patrons of the much larger St. Magdalenes must have been wealthier than those of St. Martins, Jane thought, surrounded by ornate carvings, stained windows, tracery panelling, gold-plated altars, marble memorial plaques, and tapestries edged with gold thread. She took a few moments to gaze around the church, but for all its splendour, Jane preferred the simplicity of St Martins.

As before, she walked the length of the Church, this time studying the inscriptions of the dead buried underneath the flagstone floor. She stopped to look up at a stained glass window bearing the image of a long dead patron – Augustus, Earl of Marlowe, who departed this earth on the 29th July in the year of our Lord 1598, aged forty-eight. Jane stared at the image of the man captured in glass and saw in his eyes, a mixture of power and zealotry. She could well imagine Augustus, Earl of Marlowe, ordering fallen women to be whipped six times around the churchyard before being driven out of the parish for good. Jane couldn't help wondering whether the person writing to Roz was a direct descendant of Augustus. She made a note of all names on the church notice board, as she'd done in St Martins, and left to stroll around Marlowe.

Being situated in hiker country, Marlowe had more than its fair share of outdoor shops and bed and breakfasts. The start of a very famous walk was a few minutes out of town, and as the morning wore on, Jane noticed many hikers and cyclists, carrying heavy rucksacks and wearing muddy, thick walking boots. She walked past a young couple sat in a café, demolishing a cooked breakfast, the remains of two bowls of porridge by their side. Two racing bikes, leaning up against the wall behind them, gave the clue as to how they remained enviously thin. Oh, to be so young and energetic, she thought wistfully, before turning her mind back to the matter in hand.

The cyclists and walkers made her wonder whether the letter writer might have been a holidaymaker who'd come across a photograph of Roz announcing her candidature? No, she realised, that could not be it. The letters suggested the sender might become one of Roz's constituents were she elected. An alternative scenario suggested itself. Could the sender of the letters be one of the other candidates in the election, or an overzealous campaign assistant, who'd come across the minefield which was Roz's past (although from what source, she couldn't for the moment imagine) and decided to use it against her?

She wondered if this might be a bit excessive for a local election, but then remembered Felix Dawson-Jones saying one day, "local politics are every bit as Machiavellian and underhand as any national election, Jane, believe me." He'd told her of a parish election where someone accused a rival candidate of once beating him up at primary school and stealing his lunch money – something the other candidate had felt the need to strenuously deny. "These council elections can get very heated," he'd said. "I've seen fist fights."

Jane decided this idea was as good a place to start as any. Now she came to think about it, she realised she hadn't asked which party Roz was running as a candidate for. She was surprised to discover it was the Conservative Party.

"I've always been a supporter," Roz said, after Jane telephoned her and ran her theory passed her. "It makes sense. But I don't know how they could have found out. I've never said anything to anyone."

"Often these things appear to be unfathomable, but when looked at carefully, they are in fact, quite straightforward," Jane replied.

It transpired only two other candidates were running against Roz: the Liberal Democrat Party candidate and the Green Party candidate. "The Labour Party didn't file their return on time." Roz said. "I think they did it deliberately. They know they'd lose their deposit if they fielded a candidate here."

Jane decided to visit the Liberal Democrat candidate first at their campaign headquarters, a small two-roomed office in a portacabin next to a fish and chip shop. Jane thought the candidate herself to be a perfectly charming, if a slightly scruffy woman. Her campaign team consisted of a husband and teenage daughter. Jane put the couple in their forties, which meant they would have been children when Roz was working as a prostitute. Jane introduced herself as a local resident, giving a name and address imparted to her by Roz of a local resident with the postal vote who

Roz knew spent most of her time in London, and pretended to be concerned with a small incident with a neighbour over a shared car parking space.

"I really think there should be more parking spaces," Jane said, "then there wouldn't be all these arguments," she added, getting into her part. The two women sat at a small table. While Jane spoke, the Liberal Democrat candidate took notes of Jane's concerns. A photocopier whirred continuously behind them, whilst at another table, the candidate's husband and daughter folded leaflet after leaflet, ready for an evening delivery.

"I agree there isn't anything like enough parking," the candidate agreed. "I intend to raise this as an issue at the first council meeting, should I be elected."

"I do hope so," Jane said, trying to sound irritated. "I raised this issue with the Conservative candidate but she really wasn't interested at all."

"Really?" the Liberal Democrat candidate asked. She shot a look at a husband, which suggested she found this comment surprising. He merely shrugged back. "Although I'm running against her, personally, I'm surprised to hear you say that."

"May I ask why?"

"She and her campaign team come across as hard-working and conscientious," the candidate said.

"I think it's because she's not local born and bred."

"Isn't she?" the candidate said. "I thought she was, to be honest, but I suppose now you mention it, the accent isn't from around here."

"Are you?" Jane asked.

"We both are," her husband said, from across the room. "Born and bred and raised within a gnats breath of here."

"Are your parents still alive?" she asked.

"Unfortunately both our sets of parents are dead," the candidate said. Her husband put down the pamphlet he'd been folding and walked over to his wife to ask Jane why she'd asked the question.

"I just wondered if I knew them, that's all," Jane said. "May I ask what church you regularly attend? I do believe such things are important."

Jane could tell from the look on all three of their faces, and the awkward silence which followed, that the answer was none.

"I'm not sure that any of your business," the candidate's husband eventually said.

She made her excuses and left. From there she made her way to the Green Party's headquarters. These were located above a vegan restaurant. Jane hesitated by the door. Everything on the restaurant menu sounded so delicious, and the smell emanating from it was so enticing, that Jane decided to stop for lunch before visiting the candidate.

When Jane finally met the Green Party's candidate, she found a casually dressed young man, every bit as perfectly mannered and as intense as she'd expected him to be. He even had a beard. He was young enough to be Roz's grandson, as was most of the team supporting his campaign, judging by the youngsters who kept coming in and out of the room.

When she repeated her tale of the on-going argument she was supposedly having with her next-door neighbour over a shared parking space, the Green Party's candidate response was simple.

"If there were more car parking spaces there would be more cars. As a member of the Green Party, I wish to discourage car use and encourage other forms of transport such as public transport, which I'm committed to improving."

"That's all very well, but at my age, when I have heavy shopping bags, unless a bus stops outside my house…" Jane said, getting a little too much into character. She stopped herself, remembering the reason for her visit. "Do you know the Conservative candidate?"

"I've seen her around campaigning, but not had the chance to speak to her so far."

"Do you find her a likeable woman?" Jane asked.

"I'm sure she's as likeable as any Tory," he said with a grin. "Not that I ever get close enough to a Tory to know one way or the other."

"Do you mind me asking which church you regularly attend?" she asked for the second time that morning.

This time, the look she got was not the embarrassed, bewildered one she'd received when she'd asked the same question earlier, but a rather patronising one. It was clear from the look on the young man's face that he thought Jane a silly, middle-class snob.

"I am an atheist," was the answer. "Not that it's any of your business."

"Oh, I see. What do your parents think of that, young man?" she asked, as disapprovingly as she could manage.

"They're staunch non-believers too."

"We all are," a young man said, having just walked into the room. "We don't believe in God or motorcars," he said, in a tone suggesting his comment wasn't said entirely in jest.

"I am very concerned that my area may turn into a beat for local prostitutes," Jane said.

"The Green Party support legalised brothels to protect both the women and local residents," was the pointedly non-judgemental reply.

"I see. Thank you for your time. I'll show myself out," she said, getting to her feet and walking over to the door. She left the room feeling frustrated. She was no further forward to finding the person she was looking for than she had been when she left home that morning.

As soon as she was through her front door, she logged onto the website of the Marlowe-on-the-Water Green Party and read up about the young man she'd just spoken to. Like the liberal candidate, he too was local. He'd grown up in the area and had gone to school there. He'd met his partner, Yolanda, at university, and ran the vegetarian restaurant with her. She looked at the photographs of the rest of his campaign team. Just like their candidate, they were all very young. Indeed most of them would not have been born when Roz was living and working in Greater Flyborough.

Jane didn't really see either of the candidates she'd met as being the letter writer, nor their campaign teams. She was going to have to think a bit laterally on this one. She decided to push Roz's case to the back of her mind for the time being, in the hope that her subconscious would come up with something which her conscious self had failed to spot. Her visit to the Beech Hill Art Gallery the following evening should be a nice break from things.

CHAPTER EIGHT
Spinsters Fight Back!

I

Bill Bennett stopped briefly outside the wool shop that time forgot, ran his hands through his hair, and stepped inside, where he found two of the three Bailey sisters behind the shop's long counter. He walked over to them.

"Allow me to introduce myself. My name is Bill Bennett. The council have asked me to serve you with, I mean give, you this," he said of the letter in his hand.

"You're from the council?" Nellie shrieked. "Come to evict us?"

"I'm actually what is called a process server. I've come because the council need to know you have received this letter…"

He was cut short by Nellie Bailey, running as fast as her age would allow, across the wool shop towards the door which divided it from the residential quarters, shouting: "Lettice! Lettice! We are being evicted! Man the barricades! Man the barricades!"

Bill Bennett's attempts to explain that he had not come to evict any one fell on deaf ears. Nellie disappeared through the connecting door, which she loudly locked and bolted behind her. "I haven't come to evict you," he said patiently to Dotty. "I'm only here to make sure you receive this…" He abruptly stopped speaking when Dotty emerged from behind the counter, with a pair of knitting needles in her hand. These she pointed in his direction.

51

"I want you out of my shop and my home. I'm not afraid to use these, you know," she said, jabbing the needles towards him.

At six foot three, Bill Bennett towered over the four foot nothing Dotty. He stared down on the woman in front of him. She was so small he could probably have picked her up and put her in his pocket. This didn't cow her. She advanced on him, knitting needles pointing dangerously in his direction, her tiny frame visibly shaking.

"This is still our property which you are on uninvited and unwanted. We're allowed to defend ourselves and our property. We have the law on our side."

Rather than argue with her, Bill raised his hands in a conciliatory fashion, and backed away, taking one step backwards, while Dotty took one step forward. They continued in this way until Bill reached the front door. He didn't turn his back on Dotty until he'd safely stepped outside in as calm and as dignified a way as he could manage, hoping Dotty wasn't about to chase him through the streets of Failsham, knitting needles at the ready. He was quite relieved when he heard the door locked and bolted behind him, as for only the second time in its history, the wool shop closed early.

Bill hadn't finished the task he'd been appointed to do. He bent down and opened the shop's brass letter box, pushing the letter through it, only for it to be almost immediately pushed back out again, followed by the sharp end of the knitting needles and Dotty shouting, "We will fight this all the way, the council can be sure of that. My sisters and I will be writing to the Prince of Wales himself about this!"

"What's wrong with those old ladies?" Councillor Duigan yelled down the phone to Felix Dawson-Jones, after Felix had called him to tell him about the incident with Bill Bennett. "Why do they keep attacking people who are only trying to help them?" he continued from the passenger seat of a car driven by his wife. "It's lucky for them Sarah and Bill are being so good about it. Those women should consider themselves lucky the police haven't been called."

"I don't think they view it as attacking us," Felix reasoned from his hallway. "They think they're defending their home, which in a sense they are."

"Why on earth do they want to stay in that musty old building of theirs? It's wholly illogical."

"I'm not sure logic comes into it."

"Old women!" Duigan said, derogatorily. "Well we've served the formal notices on them, if they want to leave them lying in the street that's their business. There's just the public meeting to get through, then the lawyers can take over. I should have left it all to them in the first place. No good deed ever goes unpunished," he muttered ruefully, as his car pulled into a tunnel and the line cut out.

CHAPTER NINE
Graham Burslem

Beech Hill was a steep, narrow, quaintly cobbled lane, lined by tiny and misshapen buildings preserved from mediaeval times. At its pinnacle stood a mediaeval church and a beech tree, said to be as old as both church and lane. Whilst the higgledy-piggledy nature of the bumpy, uneven cobbled lane, lent itself well to the cafés, antique shops, craft shops, and art galleries which lined it, it also made visiting rather strenuous. Thank heavens, Jane said to herself, when she realised the Beech Hill Art Gallery, stood at the bottom of the hill and not the top.

Jane peered through the gallery's window and was a little surprised to discover it empty apart from a solitary man sitting behind a desk near the door, whom she took to be Graham Burslem. She double-checked her invitation to ensure she'd arrived at the right place at the right date. She had and so she stepped inside.

Although housed in a centuries-old timber-framed building, the gallery's interior was much more modern than its exterior, having at some stage over the years, been gutted to create one large room, with living quarters above. Lit by windows which reached from ceiling to floor, with lime-washed walls, and under-floor heating, the open-plan room was light and warm.

"Now, this is lovely," Jane said to Graham Burslem.

"Thank you," he replied.

"Am I early? Or late?" she asked, glancing round the empty gallery.

Graham laughed out loud and got to his feet to pour her a glass of white wine from a bottle on the desk. He was a tall, overly thin man probably in his sixties. Jane glanced over to the lowest part of the gallery, whose ancient ceiling sloped downwards, at the same place as its floor sloped upwards, and wondered whether Graham could actually stand upright there.

The door to the gallery opened and a glamorous and rather bohemian looking young couple walked through it. Both wore ankle length velvet coats, with scarves wrapped around their necks, and dark velvet caps, with gold tassels. Unless it was Jane's imagination, Graham seemed surprised by the couple's appearance in his gallery. He stared first at them and then back to the door, as though he'd meant to lock it, but had forgotten to do so. Common sense told her that no one else but she was supposed to be there. She listened on.

"Are you the artist?" the female half of the couple asked Jane, after having scanned the gallery.

"I wish I could say yes," Jane replied.

"Unfortunately Mandy herself can't be here," Graham said of the 'young and upcoming photographer' – Mandy Tomas.

"For her own exhibition?" the young woman asked.

"Her mother was rushed to hospital this morning," Graham explained. "You can imagine how disappointed she was."

The young couple looked at each other and said they could.

"Are you her sponsor?" the young man asked.

55

Graham motioned to photographs of the human eye, which lined the walls of the gallery, and said, "I am. I absolutely love Mandy's work and will promote it to my dying day."

The couple asked whether they could look around.

"Of course, please do," Graham said.

His reply came across as unenthusiastic. The presence of the couple appeared to grate with him somewhat, although the couple didn't appear to notice this and began to bombard Graham with questions about the artist and her photographs, which he answered rather half-heartedly and briefly, something Jane thought surprising for a man who'd just stated how much he loved the artist's work.

With the couple monopolizing Graham, Jane was left to her own devices. She walked around the gallery, stopping to look at each photograph in turn, before moving on to the next. The eyes captured on film came in many shapes, sizes and colours, some more unconventional than others. Some of the eyes came in pairs, some were singles, and one was of a Cyclops. Some of the eyes were open, others closed. They winked, or were open wide in surprise, or had a beauty mark beneath them. In one photograph, a man's hand shielded his eyes; in another, an Indian caste daub separated the eyes of the young Asian woman. One eye had a deep scar running across it, making its owner unable to open it; others were so damaged by white cataracts, they rendered their owner blind. Some of the eyes belonged to children, whilst others images were of fading, elderly eyes, with drooping eyelids and heavy bags and thick deep wrinkles, etched underneath them. In some of the more unconventional pictures, the irises were painted vivid orange, or purple, or striped, or pairs of eyes had different colours. Those sold had small red stickers on their right hand corners.

Jane returned to the first photograph she'd looked at, having walked around the entire exhibition. Whilst she'd enjoyed it, in the end, the entire exhibition came across as being something hurriedly put together on a computer by an art student, keen to complete an end-of-year project before the party season kicked off and Graham's enthusiasm for the absent photographer seemed disproportionate to the talent displayed on the walls. Jane couldn't help wondering if Graham was the young photographer's father, or even her sugar daddy. Shame on you, she thought.

She heard the gallery's front door open, and turned round to see Graham showing the couple out of the gallery. This time he locked the door and put the closed sign up.

"You worried I'm going to leave without buying anything?" she joked.

Graham invited her to sit down, which she did. He topped up her glass of wine and said, "Allow me to explain."

"By explain you mean why you have really invited me here. It wasn't to try and sell me some artwork, was it?"

"No, it wasn't. It was to ask you to sell some artwork on my behalf, actually."

"Sell?" Jane said, rather surprised at the request.

"I don't know how much you know about the art world," he began.

Jane admitted she knew little.

"I'm relatively well-known in the art world, which is a small, cliquey world. What is less well-known among my associates is that I'm effectively bankrupt. I got involved in overseas property just as the market imploded. Even Jenny, my wife, doesn't know how bad things are. The only way I can repay my debts is to sell my most precious possession, a collection of sketches of a young woman by an artist called Jasper August."

Jane admitted she'd never heard of the artist. Graham explained that Jasper August was a contemporary artist of some repute who'd died of a brain tumour within the last few years, adding, "Unfortunately for Jasper, but fortunately for all those who own a piece of his artwork."

"Go on," Jane said.

"Many years ago, I shared a flat with Jasper and another man, whose name I can't remember. Bernie? Benny? Don't know. In those days, we were the ones with the money, and Jasper the impoverished one. After Jasper hadn't sold any work in ages, Bernie as we'll call him, agreed to pay his share of the rent. He couldn't see him out on the street, could he? To thank him, Jasper gave Bernie a sketch pad containing sketches of Jasper's then girlfriend, Angela. It may not seem much, but those sketches formed the basis of what would become his most famous picture – a portrait of Angela. Like every other artist I've ever known, he assured us that one day he'd be rich and famous, and Bernie would thank him for it when that day came. But unlike all the others, he actually did become rich and famous. By that stage, the three of us had gone our separate ways. What Jasper didn't know is that Bernie swapped me the sketches for my guitar. He never liked the sketches and I'd never been able to master the guitar. It seemed a fair swap at the time. I hung on to the sketches, and now Jasper's dead, they're extremely valuable. I hate to part with them, but this is about as rainy a day as it gets, and so I'm going to have to."

"And where exactly do I fit in?"

"If it becomes known that I'm selling the sketches, people will inevitably find out why. Once the real reason comes out, its price will go down. People bid low in fire sales."

"I see," Jane said. "Forgive me for seeming rather slow, but surely if it's known that the sketches are yours, how is my selling it on your behalf going to help?"

"Because nobody knows I have it. In fact, outside these walls, no one knows where the sketches are. That Jasper drew them is public knowledge, but their whereabouts remain a mystery except to you and me. Jasper, Bernie and I lost touch years ago. After he became successful, Jasper contacted me to enquire if I knew where Bernie was, and whether he still had the sketches? He wanted to buy them back. I didn't need the money, nor did I particularly want to sell them, knowing they would only increase in value. If Jasper had found out I had the sketch-pad, he'd have badgered me until I sold it back to him, so I told him I hadn't a clue where Bernie was, but I knew for a fact he'd given the sketch-pad away years earlier, well before Jasper became well-known. I said I didn't know where it was, or even if it still existed. He told me that Bernie always was a damned fool and I agreed with him."

"Good heavens!" Jane said. "But I'm still not entirely sure where I come in?"

"You will be playing the part of the owner of the sketches, who wants to sell them," Graham said. "I've prepared an ingenious story, explaining how the sketch-pad came to be into your possession and where it's been all these years. I've selected a gallery, which I know will be able to verify its authenticity. They'll almost certainly insist on getting a second opinion from independent art auctioneers such as Fonebies. They may even run tests to see if there are any of Jasper's fingerprints on it. There should be – I've always kept the pad in a zipped binder and worn gloves to handle the sketches. Feel free to leave the sketch-pad with them, but please do get a receipt for it. You'd better bring some ID with you, by the way. The independent verification shouldn't take too long. Once complete, the gallery will contact you, and undoubtedly offer to buy the sketches from you straight away. I'll tell you what their worth, and you mustn't take any less. They can pay you, and then you can pay me once the money has cleared. I'm assuming your agency has its own bank account?"

Jane nodded.

"I'm going to Germany shortly. With any luck, by the time I get back, you'll have good news for me."

Jane leant back in her chair and took a sip of wine. "I take it this exhibition isn't for real?" she asked, wondering why he'd gone to so much trouble to mount a fake exhibition, rather than simply pick up the telephone to her.

"It is," Graham said. "It's a genuine exhibition, but today is the last day. I sent Mandy home early so I could talk to you. I don't bother opening my gallery in Sailles over the winter – there's absolutely no point. No

60

tourists, the second homeowners are all back in the Home Counties, so I spend the winter months launching new artists up and down the UK. Mandy is one of them. It's her work I'm taking to Germany. I'm immensely proud of my success in promoting the careers of new artistic talent such as Mandy Tomas, particularly those trying to make it outside London."

"I'll need to do some investigations. I can't just take your word for all of this, you understand."

"I wouldn't expect anything less," Graham said. "I can assure you, my story will check out. I've even got my passport and a utility bill with my address on it to show you." He produced the documents. Jane opened the passport and studied the name and photograph on it. The passport was in the name of Graham Burslem, and the photograph in it, the man opposite her.

The passport was just under seven years old. Just as she began to make a note of the passport details, Graham said,

"Why don't you hang on to it for a few days? I don't need it immediately and you can carry out any checks you want to on it."

"Are you quite sure?" Jane asked.

"As long as I have it back before I go to Germany, I'm quite happy for you to take it, as proof of my good faith. We can meet up again at my gallery in Sailles in a week or so."

She slipped both the passport and utility bill into her handbag.

"If you don't mind I'd like to visit the library and make further investigations before I'm prepared to go any further."

"Be my guest."

She walked from the gallery to the library in less than ten minutes. She searched on-line against the artist Jasper August and read everything which came up, before typing *Angela - a portrait by Jasper August*. Everything she read confirmed Graham's story, up to a point. There was mention of the portrait's preliminary sketches having been lost, and the portrait itself as having been recently sold at auction.

Whilst she was there, Jane also checked out Graham Burslem's website, which described him as an art dealer with an art gallery in 'the picturesque coastal town of Sailles on the north Hoven Coast', open for business April-October (although trading through its webpage all year round). Jane stared at the photograph posted on the website for some time. It certainly looked like the man she'd left behind at the Beech Hill Gallery. The web page also referred to him as – *One time flatmate of the late Jasper August*. She clicked the link giving details of the Mandy Tomas exhibition and read about the exhibition she'd just visited. Graham's statement about the pride he took in promoting unknown regional artists was repeated there.

Jane thought she had enough to go on for the time being. As it seemed the gallery in London would want to hang on to Graham's sketches for a while, she'd have enough time to make any further investigations she needed to.

Once back at the gallery, she noticed a small sign to the side of the door:-

Beech Hill Art Gallery, 116 Beech Hill, Southstoft, Hoven.

For all enquiries contact Lionel Scott on...

Jane took note of both name and number, before walking back inside the gallery.

"Are the sketches here?" she asked.

His face lit up. "I hoped you'd say that."

A door to the rear of the main gallery led to a small room. There was little in the room except for an empty easel, some wooden picture frames resting against a wall, and a long table covered with a cloth. Graham lifted the cloth to reveal a blue plastic binder. After putting on some white gloves, and asking Jane to do the same, he removed the sketch-pad from its binder and allowed Jane to see sketches it contained. Most of the sketches were made by charcoal or graphite pencil, but a few were watercolours. Many were incomplete, no more than a few strokes or dabs of different colours over a pencil drawing, as the artist selected his shade. Graham stopped at the most complete watercolour in the pad. It was a portrait of a beautiful young woman of Scandinavian descent with pale blue eyes, flaxen hair cut into a neat bob, and lightly freckled skin. She sat at an angle, her head tilted, looking away from the artist. There was something elfin about her, Jane thought.

As though he could read her thoughts, Graham said. "Don't be fooled by that waif-like vision of angelic loveliness. There was nothing angelic about Angela. She was half fire-breathing dragon, and half she-wolf!" He shuddered.

"Really? She certainly doesn't come across as such in this."

"Really!" he said curtly. "Appearances can be deceptive, you know. I've printed off some details of the gallery who will buy it. Here let me fetch them for you."

He left Jane studying the sketches, and returned a few minutes later with a printout of a webpage. She hadn't had very long to read it, when he said, "I don't want to sound pushy or anything, but when would you be able to visit the gallery? I'm really quite desperate for the money, you see. It'll take time to authenticate the sketches and I've creditors threatening to put in the receiver. It's getting harder and harder holding them off, whilst putting on a brave face."

For the first time that evening, he looked vulnerable. He turned away but Jane still saw the tears his eyes.

"I can go tomorrow if you want," she said. "I'll need to drive down, if I'm to take the sketches with me. Any time in the afternoon should do it."

"I'll book an appointment for you then," he said.

She returned to her car and from there she telephoned Lionel Scott, the owner of the Beech Hill Gallery, taking the part of an amateur artist and enquiring if the gallery was available for her to show her work in. When he said it was, she asked if they could meet there in a day or two, and with an appointment arranged, she drove home, stopping on the way to call in on her friend, Ant Dillard. Ant was a lay magistrate, with a son in the police force and she thought he might be able to help.

"I need help in establishing the authenticity of a client of mine," she explained to him, after he'd invited her inside. "I know I'm breaching my duty of client confidentiality in telling you this but I can't take the risk that I might be party to a fraud."

64

"Tell me only what you need to Jane, on the understanding that everything you say will be in the strictest confidence," Ant replied.

"In that case, I won't tell you why the person concerned has instructed me only that he has and I need to make sure he is who he says he is. This is the passport of the person in question." She handed the passport to Ant. "Could you have the same checked out to ensure it isn't stolen or a counterfeit? It goes without saying I have the authority of its owner to carry out these checks, but it should remain as confidential as possible."

"Understood."

"It's a bit unorthodox, I know, but I also need to make sure there aren't any reports of any stolen Jasper August sketches, even reports made many years ago. Whilst you're at it, maybe you could ask your son to confirm the owner of the passport hasn't got any previous convictions, particularly for fraud."

"I suppose you want all this by yesterday?"

"Would tomorrow afternoon be possible?"

Ant laughed at her cheek, and promised he'd do what he could.

CHAPTER TEN
Can it Be?

The gallery Graham Burslem hoped would purchase his sketches was called the Diamond Gallery. A Diamond Gallery run by a diamond geezer, no doubt, Jane thought as she read the gallery's printout before going to bed. It was located in a side street between Marylebone High Street and Harley Street, a few minutes walk from Regent's Park. To Jane's relief, the gallery had a car park. She studied the gallery's address on her A-Z and calculated it would take her about three hours to get there, door-to-door. With her appointment at two o'clock in the afternoon, and allowing time for a pit stop, she would leave the next morning at ten a.m.

This she did, and when she pulled into the car park at the rear of the gallery, she was seven minutes early for her appointment, leaving her just enough time to call Ant Dillard.

"The ID seems to check out," he said. "The passport was definitely issued to a Graham Burslem at that address. It hasn't been reported as stolen or missing and judging by the stamps collected over the years and well worn condition, it's not a counterfeit. There aren't any reports that we could find of any stolen Jasper August sketches, and Graham Burslem's as clean as a whistle."

So far so good, she thought.

"Let's hope he didn't paint it himself in the garage," Ant said.

"Well, that's for others to establish not us, Ant," she said, thanking him for his troubles and promising to call around and collect the passport in a day or two.

She removed the still-covered sketch-pad from the boot of the car and carried it with her into the gallery. James Haley, the gallery's owner, waited for her at the door. He was about the same age as Graham Burslem, but whereas Graham had a mane of thick curly hair, and a beard, James Haley was almost bald and clean shaven. His gallery was more conventional than Graham Burslem's. Unlike the empty windows of Graham's gallery, the windows of James Haley's gallery displayed almost as many pictures as its walls did. This gallery's collection ranged from oils to still-lives. Paintings of animals hung next to religious works. There were even cartoons.

"I understand you have a collection of sketches you'd like me to value for you?" he said, in a tone of voice which gave Jane the impression that he was merely going through the motions, and didn't really expect the sketches to have much of interest about it.

"I do, yes. All the sketches are of the same young woman. The signature says the artist is a Jasper August. My research tells me he's quite well known, although I've never heard of him. There is a girl's name written across the top left-hand corner. We've always thought it said Angela," she said, the binder containing the sketchpad still in her hands.

In front of her, James Haley almost fell over. He had to steady himself by leaning on the counter. Jane could tell that it was all James could do to stop himself from snatching the binder out of her hands.

"It can't be? Surely not?" he said, more to himself than to her. "May I see them?" Although obviously trying to calm himself down, and stop the excitement from showing in his voice, he physically shook. Jane removed the sketch-pad from its binder and lay it on the counter. Without being asked to, James Haley put on a pair of gloves. He opened the pad, staring at each picture for a few minutes, before turning to the next. When we reached the watercolour, he stretched out his hand towards it, and without touching it, he allowed his fingers to trace the outline of Angela's face.

"Is it really you?" he asked the girl.

A woman stopped in the street outside, and began to study the various pictures hanging in the gallery's windows. James Haley hurried over to the door, locked it, and put the closed sign up in the window. The woman moved away.

"I don't know about you," he said to Jane. "But I need a drink. Badly."

"I wouldn't mind a cup of tea," Jane said.

"I'll pick the leaves myself, if this is the genuine article," he said. "I need some fresh air."

A few minutes later, Jane found herself in a deckchair on the gallery's patio roof garden, covered up in a blanket. A wrought iron fence ran around the edge of the roof garden to prevent unfortunate accidents. To her right, sage grew in a pot, and lavender in another. How beautiful they must smell when in bloom, Jane thought. She sipped her lemon tea contentedly. A pair of blackbirds, also enjoying the view of the rooftops of London from the branches of a tall Bay tree in the corner of the garden, chirped happily away. How quiet it is up here, Jane thought to herself – the roar of the traffic on the streets below almost inaudible.

The comfort of the blanket, combined with the aroma from the tea, and the stillness of the roof garden, meant Jane was having some difficulty staying awake.

She sat herself up in the chair, while beside her, James, also in a deckchair, drank the large whisky he'd poured himself.

"I can't believe it," James Haley said, for the umpteenth time. "I'm actually shaking in astonishment. Literally shaking. Please tell me how you came by those sketches, and then I'll tell you why I am so excited."

As she had been instructed to do, Jane told him the story prepared for her by Graham Burslem.

"They belonged to my late husband. He said he fell in love with them, or rather with their subject, the first time he saw them. This was before he met me, of course," she added. "When he was at college, someone walked into a bar with the sketches under their arm. I know money changed hands, but how much I couldn't tell you, nor who the original owner was, I'm afraid. We've always kept the sketches in some kind of protective binder, in an old chest. Now and then, my late husband would get them out to show people. He was quite proud of his purchase – she's a beautiful girl, let's be honest. Neither of us ever thought the sketches might be valuable. I came across them quite recently, and did a bit of research, leading me to believe that they might be worth something after all. I'll be very happy if they are. I won't pretend I don't need the extra money. It's so hard to make ends meet, being on one's own."

"I completely understand," James Haley said. "I'm going to have to get them validated. But if they are, what I think they are, then I'll have some very good news for you indeed. I need to make a telephone call. I'll do that now, and then I'll refresh your tea for you and tell you all about Angela."

James returned soon afterwards, with a fresh pot of lemon tea and a plate of chocolate biscuits, which he placed on the small table next to Jane. This time he too drank tea.

"Jasper August was an exceptionally talented, and unusually for his profession, an exceptionally successful and wealthy artist, who died fairly recently. Jasper was not always successful and wealthy. He struggled for success for many years. When he was still a young man going through his starving in a garret phase, he painted some sketches his girlfriend of the time which he ended up giving to a flatmate in lieu of rent, so the story goes. As is often the way of things, Jasper and flatmate drifted apart, and in the course of events, both flatmate and sketches went missing and, despite repeated pleas from Jasper, they have never resurfaced, until this moment that is." He glanced at Jane. "Jasper went on to paint a portrait of Angela which has just been bought by some rich New York financier," he explained. "I would be astonished if he didn't want to buy this collection."

"What happened to the actual girlfriend?"

"She and Jasper eventually split up and she was never heard from again either. She's probably an overweight middle-aged mother of adolescent children now, her Bohemian days as an artist's muse, long over," he said, ruefully. "The call I just made was to John Stem, the president of the Jasper August society. He's on his way here now. If anyone will be able to authenticate those sketches, it will be him."

She was relieved to find that, so far at least, the story told to her by Graham Burslem being substantiated by James Haley.

John Stem arrived within the hour, clutching a Jasper August sketch of a different woman. He was clearly as excited by the potential discovery of Angela as James Haley. After greeting Jane enthusiastically, he turned his attention to the sketches. They stood two easels side-by-side, and placed some of Jane's sketches on one, and John Stem's on the other, to compare. Jane watched on in quiet admiration, while the two men spent hours studying the sketches with magnifying glasses, peering intently at every minute detail. They shone a halogen torch on them. They compared and discussed something very continuously referred to as, 'the broad strokes technique' – a technique apparently commonly used by August. They compared his attention to fine detail, his use of shade and light, her features, the backgrounds, the variations in the details, and his signature. They noted that in the watercolour, Angela wore a simple pearl necklace. The use of a single pearl somewhere in his portraits, was a recurring feature in his work, Jane learnt that afternoon. ('His motif,' as James Haley put it). The two men stared closely at the sketches and stood some way away from them. They held some of the sketches up to the light and compared them with the others. They turned the lights off briefly, and both stood staring at the sketches in the semi-light, before switching the lights back on. Finally, a decision was made.

"I believe they'res genuine, James," John Stem declared.

"I can't disagree," James Haley said, biting into his own clenched fist.

"I'm going to call Fonebies," John Stem said.

He moved to the other side of the art gallery, and made the call to the famous art auctioneers from there. Jane watched him, exhilaration written across on his face.

"I'd better take some details from you. Oh hang that," James said, picking Jane up and swinging her around in his arms. "Thank you, thank you, thank you. I've waited all my life for a moment like this." He put her down again.

"My details," she said, passing him her passport and a notelet on which she'd written down her name and address. James gave the passport no more than a cursory glance before returning it to her. The notelet he put in the till.

"Would you object to leaving the sketches here with us for a while?" he said. "We'll need to ask Fonebies to cast their expert eye over it. I'll give you a receipt obviously. If this sketch-pad of yours is genuine, I'll give you twenty thousand pounds for it."

She hesitated. Twenty thousand pounds? Graham had said it was only worth fifteen thousand.

"Okay, okay – twenty-five thousand pounds. You drive a hard bargain for such a sweet lady."

Jane left the gallery shortly afterwards with the promised receipt, a photograph of herself and James Haley standing outside his gallery holding the sketches, and an offer on the table, ten thousand pounds higher than she'd been instructed to accept. Graham will be pleased, she thought.

How nice to have had a simple, straightforward matter to deal with for a change, Jane thought to herself, as she drove home. There'd been no one to follow, no conundrums to unravel, no clues to decipher, and she still had enough time to investigate Graham Burslem further. Now if she could crack Roz's case, she'd be happy. She wondered if Orla Wilson's case was going to be so cut and dried. She doubted it.

CHAPTER ELEVEN
Spinsters Spill the Beans!

Jane walked through the doors of one of the oldest pubs in the country, the Maidservant's Arms, at a couple of minutes past midday. Behind her came the three Bailey sisters, dressed, as always, in floral print dresses, flat pale leather shoes, thick nylon stockings (Jane wondered where they got them from, in this day and age) and each wearing her undyed hair in a neat bun at the back of her head. Mirabella, who'd swapped her cassock for a dark blue Kaftan covered with tiny white flowers, was last through the door.

Built by monks to sell their beer, the Maidservant's Arms nestled in the grounds of Southstoft's mediaeval cathedral by the banks of the river Evening. Not only was it one of the oldest pubs in the country, it was one of the smallest, with a ceiling so low, that tall men had literally to bow when inside. Its unpainted walls were rough to the touch, and its flagstone floor shiny and worn away through centuries of use. A large fire warmed it in the winter, and its flagstones kept it cool in the summer. Although the Maidservant's Arms still sold Cathedral Beer (which Jane had never been able to abide, finding it far too strong for her liking, although her late husband had enjoyed nothing more than a pint of Cathedral Beer) it wasn't the Inn's beer the party had come to sample that day, but its famous cream tea.

The party chose a table in an alcove, close to the roaring wood fire, with views over the grounds and the river. "Who could ever tire of cream tea at the Maidservant's Arms, ladies?" Mirabella asked with a pretend wistful-sigh. "Not me. Oh, will you look at that?" She pointed to the grounds outside as she spoke. "How adorable."

The group turned to look at a group of tiny primary school children being frog-marched along the cathedral footpath as it followed the river through the cathedrals grounds towards the city. The children walked hand-in-hand in pairs along the path. A teacher at the head of the line kept turning around to ensure her charges were still following her, while another at its end, kept order by barking orders at the children – telling them to hurry up, not to dawdle, not to run, not to walk too quickly, nor to walk too slowly.

"Poor things," Nellie said. "They're not allowed any fun nowadays."

"We used to love playing in the cathedral grounds when we were children," her sister Lettice said. "Our parents came quite regularly. We did so love it, didn't we girls? Oh my," she said, of the cream teas which had just arrived on a silver, three-tiered platter. The first tier was piled high with sandwiches made from white bread, cut into triangles. The second tier contained enormous fruit scones filled with cream and jam, and the third tier a whole home-made Victoria sponge. Pots of tea, in silver teapots, alongside jugs of milk and delicate china crockery and silver cutlery also appeared.

"Oh my, indeed," Jane said. "How on earth are we to eat all of this?"

"I think we will manage somehow," Mirabella said, looking as though she could single-handedly demolish the whole lot, which Jane had no doubt she could. Food was Mirabella's great love. She loved cooking, and was rarely unable to find time to cook for her family. If Mirabella wasn't cooking food, she was preparing it, buying it or thinking about it. Sometimes she even thought about food when delivering a sermon, and more than once had lost her place as a result. She knew she ate far more than was good for her. Both she and Felix were overweight, her cholesterol and B.P was too high and she was almost certainly diabetic, but you only live once, she reasoned, and whilst she knew she would have to lose weight and get some exercise eventually, as far as she was concerned, that day had not yet come.

"Shall I be mother?" she asked, holding one of the teapots in her hand and beginning to pour.

"There was a train running then," Dotty announced.

Unsure to what it was that Dotty was alluding, Jane and Mirabella glanced at each other. Realising that neither Jane nor Mirabella could have known what she was talking about, Dotty explained herself.

"The train used to run between Failsham and Southstoft, in those days, you see," she said.

"That's how we used to get to Southstoft to visit the cathedral, when we were still children," Nellie said. "We didn't have such a thing as a car. Hardly anyone did in those days. Only the rich could afford them."

"You know, I never knew there was a train between Failsham and Southstoft," Mirabella said. "Did you Jane?"

Jane said she had not.

"It was the train which still runs between the coast and London, but in those days it also stopped at Failsham," Lettice said.

"I remember when I was allowed to travel on it for the first time without our Mama or our Papa," Dotty said. "I felt so grown up. My cousin, Iris and I made a real day of it. She was to die of yellow fever only a few years later. I still miss her to this day."

A poignant silence followed, which was broken by Mirabella saying, "Do help yourself to sandwiches, ladies."

Nobody needed to be asked twice, and the sandwiches quickly moved from platter to plate. Jane took a bite from her cucumber sandwich. This is what she loved about the Maidservant's Arms – it was a trip back in time, something quite appropriate for a day out with the Bailey sisters.

"I remember my daughter playing Pooh sticks with her father from that bridge. She was so little, she had to be picked up to be able to drop her stick over the edge. I can't remember who won," Jane said.

"Talking about childhood, you promised to show me some photographs, ladies," Mirabella said, kindly.

"Oh you do indulge us, you really do," Nellie said, giggling. With help from Mirabella, she took a photograph album out of her bag. It was too big for her to hold, and therefore she laid it on the table. Inside were tiny black and white photographs, cut up from larger photographs to form a montage, crowded together on the page. Her hand shaking slightly, Nellie turned its pages, "This is our mother as a five-year-old with her parents," she explained, her old gnarled hand resting on a photograph of a young couple and their little girl. The man, dressed formally in a dark morning suit and stood slightly behind his younger wife, came across as aloof and distant. The sisters' grandmother, equally formally attired in heavy ankle length dress and coat, rested her hand on the shoulder of a smiling little girl.

"And this handsome young man…" Dotty said, her hands also swollen with arthritis, pointed to a photograph of a man in his early twenties. "… is our dear Papa."

Jane looked at the photograph of a young man with a full head of hair, and a moustache.

"He fought in the First World War, but didn't speak about what happened to him to anyone, not even to Mama," Lettice said. "He was a signal man on the railways. Signals had to be changed manually then. They were as big as a man, you know," she said, miming signals being pulled forward or backwards.

Every page contained more montages, mostly of the sisters as children, or young women dressed in the fashion of the day. In one, Lettice was dressed in a white lace cotton knee length dress and holding a white lace parasol, lent against the bumper of a Bentley next to a young man wearing a tweed suit, his arm around her.

"His name was Alfred Foraker and he was Lettice's beau," Dotty explained. "She was the only one of us girls who came close to marrying, but Alfred died in the Second World War and that was that."

"His elder brother was killed forty-eight hours later, leaving a widow and two children. They were buried side-by-side," Lettice said.

"We still visit his grave on his birthday…" Nellie said. "…to tend it. It's not far from here."

"He was not yet twenty-six when he died," Lettice said, her voice so low it was almost inaudible.

"Lettice, I had no idea, I really didn't," Jane said, reaching across the table to take the old lady's hand in hers.

"Neither did I," Mirabella said, wiping the tears from her eyes and blowing her nose.

Nellie turned a page and a sketch fell out. Jane picked it up. The portrait was of a young couple sat astride a penny farthing, laughing and clearly very much in love. Jane asked who the couple were.

"Our mother's mother's parents. There weren't any photographs of them, the photographs of our parents are the oldest photographs in the book. Mama sketched them from memory. Mama was such a good artist. She used to sell her pictures in the market. Only Nellie has inherited her artistic talent. She used to display her paintings, didn't you Nellie dear?" she said to her sister, to which Nellie raised her hand to her face in embarrassment.

Another picture showed their parents helping out in a soup kitchen.

"It was the depression. People who had, gave to people who hadn't," Lettice explained simply.

"You must have lots of stories of village life to tell," Jane said. "Quite a few of them scandalous, I'll bet."

"Oh we do," Lettice said.

"Oh do tell," Mirabella said wickedly.

The sisters glanced at each other.

"Well, there was Amelia, Lady Hoven, the squire's wife," Dotty explained. "She loved her heirs and graces that one, but she was no better than many of those she liked to look down her nose at, when all was said and done."

Nellie took up the story. "She got herself involved with an Arthur Carter – an out and out rogue if ever there was one – the stories we could tell you about that family would make your hair curl."

"He once stole some of our coal from our coal scuttle," Dotty interrupted, "I saw him run away from the garden myself with a bag of our coal under his arm. I gave chase and he dropped the coal."

"We went straight to the police," Lettice said. "But they said we were mistaken in our identification. Their investigations proved him to have been at the Winter Fair the whole time. They told us many people swore to having seen him there. He even participated in a wrestling match according to them and so nothing ever came of it naturally, but we know it was him who tried to steal our coal, and we know how he did it."

"How?" Mirabella asked.

"He went to the fair, strolled around as big as brass drawing attention to himself, slipped away, stole a horse, rode to Failsham, did his thieving, and rode back again in time for his wrestling match," Nellie said triumphantly.

"My word," Mirabella said. "What happened between this scoundrel and Lady Amelia?"

"Well, Lady Amelia got herself involved with Arthur Carter…" Dotty said.

"… and when Carter's wife had a baby more than a few eyebrows were raised," Lettice said. "They'd been married nay on eighteen years and produced nothing, then this boy arrived."

"It couldn't have been Carter's wife who gave birth to that boy. She was past her time for that kind of thing," Nellie said.

"There were rumours of course, Lady Amelia hadn't been seen for months beforehand, but no one could ever prove a thing. All I'll say on the subject, is if there was ever a human being who was a cross between his parents it was that boy," Lettice said disdainfully.

"Is Arthur Carter still alive?" Mirabella asked.

"Long dead we're happy to say," Lettice informed the party.

"Carter's son wasn't the only one whose birth caused a stir. There was Clive Wilberforce's son," Nellie said. "Old Clive had married the baker's daughter, but the only birds he was ever interested in were those pigeons of his, and so his wife started spending a lot of time at the ironmongers."

"Never known a horse lose so many shoes," Dotty sniggered.

"So, when his son was born not looking a bit like his father, we all knew who and we all knew why," Lettice said.

"My word," Mirabella said. "You should record all these lovely stories of yours somehow or, and forgive me for saying this, they will die with you. I have a blog for the rectory. Many of my parishioners blog on subjects which are important to them. They talk to people all over the world. I'm sure my son could set you up with your own blog or some type of video link and that way you can share your memories with the whole world."

"You may have to change some of the names, though," Jane felt the need to point out.

Mirabella finished eating a scone, piled high with cream and jam, and turned her attention to the slice of Victoria sponge on her plate. She eyed it greedily, before taking a mouthful.

"Is that as nice as it looks, Rector?" Dotty said.

"It's quite delicious, you must all try a slice," Mirabella replied, placing a slice on each of the sisters' plates.

Jane looked out of the window. In the grounds outside, a young father and his two young children flew a bright yellow kite, which the family's retriever tried to catch by jumping up and down in the air after it. Jane could only laugh. Everyone turned to look at the family and their dog, still barking and snapping at the airborne kite high above him. In that moment the past, and the uncertain future, were temporarily blotted out, leaving those at the table happy to enjoy the present.

CHAPTER TWELVE
The Good Bergers of Failsham

Their cream tea over, and with the public meeting on the redevelopment of the market square about to start, Jane returned to Failsham where she dropped Mirabella and the Bailey sisters outside its old Primitive Methodist Chapel, whilst she went to make a quick telephone call. Something had occurred to her when looking at the photograph of the Bailey sisters' parents helping at a soup kitchen. Churches often provided soup kitchens for the homeless and the type of working girl Roz had once been. Maybe that was the connection all along? Why hadn't she thought of it earlier, she asked herself as she called Roz.

"Are you able to talk?" she asked.

"Go on," Roz said.

"Did you ever have anything to do with any churches in your Flyborough days? Did you regularly eat at a soup kitchen in one, for example?"

"I did, yeah," Roz said. "I used to eat in a soup kitchen in a church called St. Cuthberts. I was married there too, but not to my current hubby, obviously. The vicar and his missus were okay. They never preached. You don't think it was one of them, do you? They seemed so nice, but then you never can tell."

"We must rule nothing out. Do any names from St. Cuthberts come to mind?"

"'Fraid not. The drugs I was doing back then, it's amazing I can still remember my own name."

Well that was useful, Jane thought. She put her phone away and returned to the Primitive Methodist Chapel, buoyed by this revelation.

The meeting room was almost full. Most of the seats reserved for the public had already been taken, forcing some to stand at the back of the room. Mirabella and the sisters were at the front. They'd kept a seat for her. As Jane walked towards them, she noticed her neighbours, twenty-four-year-old Charity Parsons, and Charity's thirteen-year-old kid brother, Jack, at the back of the room. She waved at them and they waved back. Jane sat next to Mirabella, and smiled as reassuringly as she could manage at the sisters. She looked up at Felix, sat with the other council members on a platform facing the public. He looked extremely uncomfortable. A man with an electronic notebook and curser in hand, lent against the side of the room, ready to report back to his local newspaper, and Felix kept glancing nervously in his direction.

Councillor Duigan got to his feet and waited for the noise in the room to reduce. He was dressed, as always, in his tweed jacket, patched at the elbows, over corduroy trousers. "I formally declare this meeting open," he said before reading from a pre-prepared statement. "On behalf of the district council, I would like to announce that the council wishes to proceed with the proposed redevelopment of the market square in accordance with the plans available for inspection in the council offices."

Oh do stop being so pompous, Duigan, Jane thought to herself, as she watched him from the audience. She couldn't help wondering how a man so disengaged from his electorate had ever managed to get elected in the first place. His must be a safe seat, she thought.

"The council wishes to redevelop the centre of Failsham on the following grounds," Duigan continued. "One: that the redevelopment is for the overall benefit of Failsham by introducing more retail units and jobs. Two: that through the introduction of such retail units and jobs, the public will be encouraged to shop locally. Three: that the redevelopment will provide the council with much-needed revenue. Four: that the aforementioned revenue will be used by the council to improve the infrastructure of the area. Five: that the developer has agreed with the council to build a skate park on the currently derelict site on the outskirts of Failsham, which is something I understand, the young people are very much interested in. I would like to add that as someone who has, on more than one occasion, almost been knocked off their feet by skateboarders, I would also like to see a skateboard park safely out of town. I would like to emphasise that the council believe the redevelopment is essential if the town and the local region are to survive and prosper."

On these words, Councillor Duigan sat down, leaving Jane rather more impressed with both him and the case for redevelopment, than she would have liked to be. Judging by the loud applause in the room, it seemed she wasn't alone in this. The people had heard his words and they had liked them, she realised.

"I now invite comments from the floor," Duigan said.

Nellie Bailey slowly got to her feet. "I wish to speak on behalf of myself and my sisters," she said. The room fell silent and everyone turned to look at her. "My sisters and I have instructed lawyers on our behalf," she continued to applause. This grew as she said, "My sisters and I are going to fight this with every breath in our bodies."

"I have the letter from your lawyer in front of me," Councillor Duigan said, holding the letter up for all to see. "I must remind you that the council has offered to re-house you."

"We don't want to live anywhere else," Nellie said, stamping her foot in exasperation. "Moving from our home at our age would kill us."

Dotty also got to her feet. "Everywhere we look familiar to us. We know each and every nook and cranny of that house and each nook and cranny has a story to tell that only we know. If you bulldoze our home down, you bulldoze our lives and memories with it."

A woman from the audience got to her feet. "I don't think it fair to evict the old ladies. I wouldn't want it on my conscience if anything happened to them because they were forced to move out of their home."

"As a local shopkeeper," a different man said, standing to speak from the floor. "I would welcome anything which brings trade into town."

"That side of the square is in a terrible state. Theirs is the only property occupied now the squatters have gone. It needs something doing to it," a woman said.

"I love buying wool from the old ladies," someone else said. "Their shop is so old worldly. We can't lose it."

"Yeah, well people like you would have us all living by candlelight like the old biddies do," someone replied angrily.

Jane heard the sisters give a little start. They'd believed that everyone would side with them, but were unfortunately having to learn otherwise.

"We do not live by candlelight," Dotty said. "We have had electricity for many years now."

Jane and Mirabella looked at each other knowingly. The property did have electricity, but it ran through cables still on the outside of the wall to large round-holed plugs, leaving Jane and everyone who knew them, wondering how on earth the sisters found any electric appliances to fit.

Jane watched on in silence as the people in the hall argued on. The proposed redevelopment had divided the local region, as it had divided the Dawson-Jones's. She admired the sisters' fighting spirit, but she wasn't sure it would be enough. She felt so sorry for them. They were elderly and, despite the brave face they were putting on things, terrified. Beside her, she heard them whimpering as the argument in the hall raged on. The woman who had said she liked buying her wool from the shop, got back on her feet to address the three ladies.

"Don't allow the people in this room to bully you into leaving," she said. "The whole town isn't represented by those in this room. Organise a campaign, get people on your side."

Jane had no doubt she would have continued, had someone else not shouted out, "Oh do sit down and shut-up love."

Councillor Duigan got to his feet again.

"Ladies and gentlemen," he said. "We have heard your comments. We will now consider them. Thank you for your attendance."

As people got to their feet, Lettice's distinctive voice was the last to be heard: "We will chain ourselves to the counter, we will, rather than see our home demolished."

CHAPTER THIRTEEN
Neighbours Divided

Charity and Jack lived at End Cottage, Cuckoo Tree Lane, in the last of a row of eighteenth century labourers' cottages. A wooden fence divided their property from Jane's neighbouring cottage. With both their parents dead, Charity had assumed full parental responsibility for Jack.

"Those poor old ladies. Being kicked out of their home to make way for some new shop units. It's just not right," Charity said, while they walked home from the meeting.

Whilst his sister may have been completely opposed to the proposed redevelopment, Jack had different ideas and said so. "I don't know. We could do with some more shops. I have to get the bus to Southstoft if I want to get anything decent. And we'll get a skateboard park."

"Whose side are you on, young man?"

"There's nothing for young people to do in Failsham. A skateboard park would be wicked."

"Wicked," Charity mimicked.

"My point is a valid one," Jack said bravely. "What might be an unpopular decision for the Bailey sisters, might be a very popular decision for others, me included."

Charity ignored him.

"Galvanizing public opinion against the redevelopment might not be as easy as you think," he continued, quoting something he'd heard someone else say.

"Haven't you any homework to be getting on with?" Charity snapped as she unlocked the front door of their house.

"Only my history project," he said, grimacing.

"We'll get on with it then."

"It's got to be on something local, and I can't think what," Jack said, kicking the door.

"Do that again and I'll buy a can of paint and stand over you when you repaint it."

Sometime later, Jane pulled into her drive to find Jack on her doorstep. She got out of her car and walked over to him.

"All right?" she asked.

"No," he said. "Charity shouted at me and I can't think what to do for my history project. It's got to be about something local and I can think what."

"What about writing something on the history of the old wool shop? Those old ladies have some lovely stories about Failsham and its former residents, which most definitely deserve to be recorded somewhere. It's certainly topical."

"What's that mean?" Jack replied.

CHAPTER FOURTEEN
Sailles

I

Jane awoke with two appointments ahead of her: the first at the Beech Hill Art Gallery with its owner, Lionel Scott, and the second with Graham Burslem in his gallery in Sailles.

Before she left for the first, she decided to carry out a few more checks, beginning with an on-line search against Mandy Tomas. She easily found the artist's social networking page which confirmed she was a young artist local to the area. Mandy also used her website to sell her photographs.

Jane then carried out a search at the UK Land Registry to establish the legal ownership of the Beech Hill Art Gallery. The register gave its owner as a Lionel James Scott of the Beech Hill Art Gallery, 116 Beech Hill, Southstoft, Hoven.

Finally, with Roz's case still in mind, she searched against the Church of St. Cuthberts, Greater Flyborough. Not surprisingly, given the years which had passed and the distance between the churches, none of the names on her Marlowe list matched any of the names on the St. Cuthbert's website. She needed the names of those involved with St. Cuthberts back in the 1970s. Mirabella might be able to get hold of the Church of England's records for the time, but they would only really tell her who was employed by the church back then. That might not be wide enough. There must have been volunteers who would not be included in those records, but who might be the culprit. She needed to speak to someone there at the time, in the hope they might point her in the right direction. She'd speak to the current vicar and take it from there. She telephoned the church and made an appointment to see him the next day.

II

She arrived at the Beech Hill Art Gallery to find it showing an exhibition of paper lanterns, handmade by a local art student, and coastal scenes painted by another local artist. Rather than go straight in, she went to the cafe next door and ordered a coffee. While the girl behind the counter prepared it, Jane asked, "I was hoping to have a look around the Mandy Tomas exhibition I thought was on at the art gallery next door, but it isn't on any more, I must've missed it. It consisted entirely of photographs of the human eye apparently."

"It did," the waitress said. "I saw it through the window. Like you I meant to go in, then all of a sudden it wasn't there anymore. Shame really. I should've known better, the exhibitions change all the time there. Two pounds please."

Jane paid for the coffee, and took it with her to the hairdressers on the other side of the gallery. To her surprise a large Amanda Tomas photograph of a pair of eyes peering out from behind a long fringe, hung on its walls. The receptionist waited for her to speak.

"Did you get that from the art gallery next door?" Jane asked.

"We did. The manager quite liked it and bought it for the wall."

"I was hoping to buy one as well, but it's showing another exhibition."

"The artist's name's Amanda something," the receptionist said, walking over to study the photograph. "Amanda Tomas," she read from a card at the right hand base of the frame, which gave Amanda's name and web-address (the social networking site Jane had already visited). "I think there are more contact details on the back." She turned the picture over and on its rear side was the web address and telephone number of the Sailles' Art Gallery. Jane pretended to make a note of them.

"Did you want to make a hair appointment?" the receptionist asked.

"Maybe another day," Jane said, hurriedly leaving.

When she eventually pulled open the door of the Beech Hill Art Gallery, the two artists whose work the gallery displayed, smiled at her then hesitated, wondering whether to approach her or let her wander around.

"Would either of you be the owner, Lionel Scott?" she asked. When both shook their heads, she continued, "I'm meant to be meeting him here."

"Coming, coming," a voice called out, as someone hurried downstairs.

Lionel Scott turned out to be young, and thought Jane, extremely good-looking. After introducing themselves, the two spent a few minutes discussing rates and the gallery's availability.

"Three months time?" Jane said. "Well that at least gives me a date to aim for. Why don't I have a think about it and get back to you?" adding casually, "it was Graham Burslem who suggested I exhibit here. Do you know the Graham Burslem I mean?"

"From Sailles?"

Jane nodded.

"Yes – I've known Graham for years. He shows different artists here almost every year."

"I think he has an exhibition due to start next week, doesn't he?" Jane asked.

"Last week actually. Finished a day or two ago."

"That's right, last week, silly me. Anyway, I'll be in touch."

Just before she left, she stopped in the doorway and said, "If I'm to hand over a deposit I'll need some form of ID from you. It's just my husband says in this day and age, I should never hand over money without being certain who I'm handing it to." She tried to sound embarrassed at asking.

"Your husband is a sensible man," Lionel Scott said, taking out his wallet and removing his photo-card driving licence from it. He it held out for Jane to read. All details matched.

III

When Jane eventually arrived at the fishing port and beach resort of Sailles, on the north Hoven Coast, she still had enough time to pay a discreet visit to Graham Burslem's home, before her arranged rendezvous with him at the gallery.

Graham Burslem lived in a large, old house, on the outskirts of town, set back from the road, with a sweeping carriage drive leading to a garage, and a large front garden. A tall hedge shielded the property and the garden from the road. A car was parked in the drive. Jane parked on the other side of the road before returning on foot to peer through the hedge. It wasn't long before a woman emerged from the house and got into the car. Jane wondered if she was Jenny Burslem, as she'd be about the right age to be Graham Burslem's wife.

Jane reached her own car, just as the woman drove away. The postman arrived moments later, giving her the opportunity to use an idea she'd read about on the blog of another private detective. As soon as the postman left the property and disappeared down the neighbour's drive, she drove down the driveway and parked outside the house, hidden from view by the hedge. From her boot she removed a long pole with a device to pick up rubbish at its end. A quick peek through the letterbox revealed three letters lying on the doormat. She pushed the pole through the letterbox, and after a couple of attempts, picked up the letters. This was about as underhand as she got. The first of the letters was addressed to a Mr and Mrs G. Burslem; the second to Mrs Jenny Burslem, and the last to a Mr Graham and Mrs Jenny Burslem. She pushed the unopened letters back through the letterbox, and returned to her car. She drove to the other side of the road and parked there. After some time, the woman she'd seen leave earlier, returned to the property. Jane gave it a few minutes before telephoning the house. A woman answered.

"Am I speaking to a Mrs Jenny Burslem?" Jane asked.

"You are, yes. How can I help you?"

"I wondered if you'd be interested in taking part in a blind tasting of..."

Mrs Burslem interrupted her. "I'm terribly sorry but no."

"What about your husband?" Jane said hurriedly.

"No, I don't think so, I'm sorry," and the call ended.

From there Jane drove to the town centre. She parked at the top of the narrow high street and walked down hill to Sailles' picturesque pebble beach, glad she'd wrapped up warmly against the cold.

Jane didn't wonder Graham Burslem closed his gallery for the winter months. Sailles was a summer resort, no one came to it in February. Hardly anyone was around, and fewer still on the promenade, where the gallery was situated. The biting wind seemed to have even kept most locals at home, although Jane did notice a hardy family at the end of the promenade attaching bacon fat to a crabbing line. The wind blew stronger and she turned her collar up, just as a siren rang out, alerting anyone on the sand dunes to the rapidly approaching high tide.

As she reached the gallery, a large wave hit the concrete promenade, showering her with sea spray. She looked over to the family. They'd escaped the wave, but their bucket hadn't and rolled along the promenade, chased after by all five of them.

Jane peered inside the empty gallery. Graham hadn't arrived yet. A few coastal scenes hung on its walls, but little else. The till had been removed. A notice on the door declared it closed until the end of April. In a framed newspaper clipping, displayed in the gallery's window, Graham Burslem – described as the owner of the Sailles' Art Gallery – held an award for his work in promoting new artists. She studied the newspaper clipping closely. Although only captured from the waist up, the man in it was the man she'd met at the Beech Hill Art Gallery. Jane couldn't help noticing he'd picked exactly the same tie to wear the day she met him as he wore in the photograph. She laughed.

While waiting for him to arrive, Jane crossed the promenade and watched the crabbing boats return with the high tide, ready to unload their snapping cargos. Even though the waves crashed noisily against the promenade and the pebble beach, she could still hear the revolving blades of the windfarm (said to be the largest on the planet) far out to sea, where once stood gas rigs. She turned to watch the family. They'd retrieved their bucket, and whilst their mother filled it with sea water, the shrieking children hurled their baited crabbing lines into the sea, assisted by their father. Jane smiled remembering similar days out when she'd been a young mother.

"Jane," she heard someone call out. She looked around and saw Graham Burslem hurrying down the promenade. She returned to the gallery at the same time as he reached it. "Sorry I'm late," he said, unlocking the gallery door as he spoke.

She tried to follow him inside, but he raised a hand to stop her. "Have to turn the burglar alarm off first," he said, pressing a keyboard above the gallery's door. "All clear," he said, motioning to her to join him.

"I saw you. At my house," he said, "helping yourself to my post."

"You were there?"

"I was watching you from an upstairs window. I'm glad my wife didn't catch you," he laughed.

"So am I. I must give you your passport back," she said, taking it out of her handbag alongside the bill, and passing both to him. "They and you both check out."

97

"Glad to hear it."

"As far as I'm concerned if Fonebies authenticate the sketches then I'm prepared to sell them on your behalf."

He offered her his handshake. "They will," he said. As he spoke, his eyes turned to rest on a small oil painting of Sailles' beach. He crossed the room, removed the picture from the wall and returned to hand it to Jane.

"I couldn't possibly," she said.

"Please," he said. "I want you to have it. You can't imagine what a weight this is off my mind. All this sneaking around behind people's backs isn't doing my ulcer any good."

Jane took the picture and thanked him, leaving a few minutes later with the wrapped picture under her arm.

On the way back to her car, she called into a delicatessen she'd passed on the high street and bought herself a Sailles' crab quiche for her supper.

CHAPTER FIFTEEN
Time to put aside Childish Things

Whilst Jack could see the logic of choosing the history of the Failsham wool shop as the subject of his local history project, he was worried he might end up the butt of everyone's jokes if he turned up at school and announced his history project was about a wool shop run by three old ladies who, in the eyes of his school friends, were probably as old as the shop itself.

Then there was the skateboard park. If Failsham couldn't have the wool shop and the skateboard park, he knew which he preferred. There was also Polly to think of. Polly was a girl in his class he quite liked. She was pretty and popular. He thought she quite liked him, but he wasn't sure enough to pluck up the courage to ask her out. What would she think about his choice of project? She might want a skateboard park and think he didn't. Also, wool shops weren't very macho, and he didn't want Polly thinking he was a dork. But then local history wasn't very macho, unless it was about wars, and he didn't think Polly would be interested in wars, not that he could think of any wars involving Failsham other than the world wars, which they'd already studied.

He was running out of time. If he didn't pick a subject quickly, he wouldn't have anything to hand in at all. If he didn't hand something in, he'd fail history. Polly didn't fail anything. Polly was a grade 'A' student. Her project was probably well in hand. What was worse, he thought. Polly thinking he was a geek, or one away from being a dropout? The indecision was killing him, and the more he thought about it, the worse it was getting. He'd learned all about hormones at school, and what they did to the body, but this was worse than anything he'd been warned about.

He wondered what Johnny would have to say on the subject. Johnny was Charity's ex-boyfriend. They'd split up, after he'd decided to go travelling around the South Atlantic on the spur of the moment. Charity had cried for weeks after he'd left, as had Jack, but unlike Charity, his crying had been done in private. Once, Jane had found him crying at the end of the garden. She'd sat beside him, and explained that Johnny acted the way he did because he'd suffered a dislocated and unsettled childhood. His behaviour didn't mean he didn't love or care for Jack and Charity, but sometimes damaged people took their anger out on other people, without meaning to. She'd said something about him being wary about making attachments. Jack was sure Jane was right, but (as Charity said) knowing that didn't help a great deal. Jack missed Johnny at moments like this more than at any other. He wondered if he should call him. Johnny'd said he could: "Despite this thing with your sister, I'm still here for you, mate. You ever want advice, or just a chat, get in touch."

Johnny would be more use to him than his sister, for sure. Since the split, her advice on involvement with the opposite sex began and ended with the words: "Don't do it unless you want your heart put through a mincer, that is."

He sent Johnny a text. Johnny replied immediately. 'I think your choice of subject matter shows your sensitive side. Girls like that. Go for it, mate!'

That did it. The history of the Failsham wool shop would be the subject of his local history project.

Jack called in at the wool shop on his way to school, to run the idea past the three old ladies. They were carrying newly delivered Shetland wool, two balls at the time, from the shop's counter to the cubicles. The old ladies simply loved Jack's idea.

"Is it okay, if I pop back after school and ask you some questions and maybe take some pictures?" he asked. "You can tell me everything you know about the shop and its history. Afterwards, I'll go to the library and see what else I can find out, maybe fill in any gaps and stuff. We'll see how far back we can take it, if you like," he said.

Dotty told him they would be delighted. "You must come to tea and bring a friend," she said.

Jack invited Charity. She was happy to go along, out of curiosity more than anything else. She'd never been inside the famously 'frozen-in-time' wool shop, although she'd heard all about it from those who had, including Jane.

When the visitors arrived, the ladies clucked and cooed over them, and ushered them into the parlour, where a jug of lemonade, a pot of tea, a home-made egg and ham pie, bread and butter, pickled onions and the remains of a fruit cake, were spread out on the table, waiting to be served.

"We are flattered that two young people have chosen to pay us old ladies a visit," Lettice said.

"And honoured that you have chosen our little wool shop for your school project," Nellie said. "Aren't we girls?"

Jack was armed with his camera as well as a notebook. If his project was any good, he would put it on his social networking page.

"It's sort of like television, only you can talk to everyone who's watching at the same time," Charity explained, when asked by his sisters what social networking was.

"How wonderful," Dotty said.

"We don't really watch television. We only have one to watch the service from the Cenotaph and the Queen's speech on Christmas Day," Nellie said, motioning towards the corner of the room. Both Charity and Jack stared in amazement at the enormous 1950s wooden framed television, with a minute screen, which stood there.

"Fooled you!" Lettice said. "That thing hasn't worked for thirty years, we just haven't arranged for anyone to call around and collect it. We watch a portable."

"Maybe I could start by asking you what you know about the history of the shop," Jack said, turning over the pages of his notebook and licking his pencil, as he'd seen a detective do in an old film, although he didn't know why the detective did it, as it tasted awful.

"Ask away, dear," Dotty said.

The questioning took about an hour in total, during which Jack took copious notes. By the time he'd asked all his questions, the tea had gone cold and all the food had been eaten.

"Would you like to look around the rest of the building?" Dotty asked.

Until the tour commenced, Charity hadn't entirely believed the stories she'd heard about the wool shop's antiquity, but by the end of it, she was convinced that if she'd walked around it a hundred years earlier, she wouldn't have been able to see any difference. It certainly hadn't been redecorated in the last century that she could tell.

The cast-iron beds in the old ladies' bedrooms were covered in home-patched quilts. Each room contained a dressing table with a mirror. Lace draperies covered both dressing and bedside tables. On each dressing table there was a silverback hairbrush and mirror, tiny cut-glass bottles with silver tops, and a china jug and bowl set, and more dried flowers. Rugs covered the bare floors. The bathroom was no more modern. A copper water heater over the bath provided hot water. The bathroom's stone basin was old and stained. It's five-starred taps large and cast-iron. The toilet still had a chain flush. Charity couldn't see how they still managed to get in and out of the old cast-iron roll-top bath tub, complete with brass legs. They probably couldn't, she decided, hence the jugs in each room. The tour ended where it began, in the wool shop.

Jack took a photograph of the sisters behind their counter, surrounded by the balls of wool and decided to make the picture his project's cover page.

"Before you came, I found this," Nellie said, pushing a faded photograph of the exterior of the shop across the counter towards Jack. "It was taken by our father. You can see how different the shop is today from how it was then."

Charity and Jack both had the same thought. How was it different?

The sisters had also dug out some of the old leather-bound ledger books, kept by their father and grandfather. These large, heavy, leather bound books, recorded every purchase made. The books were laid out on the counter of the wool shop for Jack to study.

"Listen to this, Charity," he said, reading an extract out loud. "Wool (assorted colours) six balls. Mrs Lambert 2/-."

"I can still remember serving Mrs Lambert," Lettice said. "She came in every first Monday in the month and always purchased six balls of wool in various colours. She had been a widow nigh on forty years by then. We never saw her dressed in anything other than black. Even her handkerchiefs and jewellery were black. We used to be rather frightened of her when we were children, weren't we girls?" Lettice asked her sisters. "But once she started giving us gobstoppers and Papa told us she was knitting socks for the soldiers at the front line, we realised what a nice lady she was."

"Did you get all that mate?" Charity asked. "I think that's a really lovely story. I'm sure lots of people would love to hear it."

Jack made a quick note of Mrs Lambert's ledger book wool purchase in his notepad and then turned his camera on the ladies.

"Could you please repeat that story for the camera, Miss Bailey," he asked.

"And any other stories like that, if you've got them," Charity said.

In the end, it was to be another two and a half hours, plus another jug of lemonade and some homemade biscuits later, when Charity and Jack eventually left the shop. For both, entirely engrossed in the memories shared by the three old ladies, time had flown by.

"Don't say I said this," Jack said, on the way home, "but that was really interesting."

"Think you've got enough there for your project?"

"Not half," Jack said. "I think I'll go to the library tomorrow and read up on local history, though. I might find something about the shop that happened so long ago even the Bailey sisters don't know about it. Like what it was like before their parents ran it."

CHAPTER SIXTEEN
Hilda Lawley

Jane caught the train from Southstoft, for the twenty minute journey to Greater Flyborough, where she was to visit St. Cuthberts, the church once frequented by Roz. As she stared out of the train window she thought about her last visit to Greater Flyborough. Then she'd driven past a man she, and everyone else, had thought dead. When she'd told the police she'd seen him, they hadn't believed her, until she'd produced the living man and enough information to help them solve a murder. Today's visit, she hoped, would be much less adventurous.

While the train cut through scenic flat Fenland dotted with the wind pumps, isolated farm cottages, and small groups of cattle huddled together, Jane rehearsed the reasons she'd composed for her interest in St. Cuthberts. If this trip was unsuccessful, she'd have to get hold of the latest census for Marlowe on the Water, and compare it with the census for Greater Flyborough for the years in question, and see if she could compile from them a list of people who were now older than fifty, and whose names appeared on both. However, even this would not bring her much further forward, if a number of similar names appeared on both, particularly as she still didn't know the gender of the person writing to Roz. The train, she realized, was drawing into Greater Flyborough station.

Less than thirty minutes after stepping on the train, Jane was in the vestry of St. Cuthberts, with its vicar. "I have an interest in family history," she began. "Through my research I have discovered that one of my relatives faked his own death and reinvented himself by starting a new life elsewhere. I believe he created an entirely new identity for himself, to the extent that he ended up as the vicar of St. Cuthberts sometime in the 1970s."

"My word!" the vicar said. "What on earth made him go to such trouble?"

"Got a girl in trouble and fled."

"My word!" the vicar repeated. "I didn't realise the 1970s was so puritanical. I'm afraid I won't be able to help you personally. I was born in the 1970s and don't know anything about what happened at the church before my wife and I were posted here, and that was only about six years ago. I believe I do know someone who might be able to help you though – Hilda Lawley. She's the widow of Alfred Lawley, who was the vicar of St. Cuthberts between 1973 and 1978. Alfred Lawley was a local man, so he wasn't your relative. It may have been his predecessor. If anyone can help you find that out, it will be Hilda. Let me telephone her for you, and see if she might be willing to talk to you. If you're happy to wait, I could call her now?"

Jane thanked him and said she was more than happy to wait.

"Hilda says she's more than willing to help," the vicar informed Jane, once he'd come off the phone from Hilda Lawley. "She suggested you call on her straightaway, if that fits in with your schedule."

"It certainly does," Jane said, getting to her feet.

"I thought it would," the vicar said, smiling. "I've written down directions to her bungalow for you. Have you driven?"

"I'm on foot."

"In that case, it's only a few minutes down the road. She moved to a small bungalow within walking distance of the church, following her husband's death."

Jane took the piece of paper, which contained directions to Hilda's house, from the vicar and thanked him for his kindness. It took her only a few minutes to walk from the church to the bungalow, where Hilda waited for her at the front door.

Hilda wasn't at all what Jane had expected. Rather than the starched, blue-rinsed, matronly-type of woman, Jane had expected to meet, Hilda, who was about ten years older than her, was auburn-haired, nicely tanned and stylishly dressed in a colourful, striped dress.

"Thank you so much for agreeing to speak to me, Mrs Lawley. May I say what a lovely tan you have."

"That's because I've just come back from a fortnight in Turkey."

As she had many times since she'd become a private detective, Jane found herself invited to sit in someone else's living room to partake of tea and biscuits.

"How can I help you, my dear?" Hilda asked.

Over a pot of Earl Grey tea and cream puffs, with the afternoon sun pouring through the front window, Jane repeated her story. Although Hilda listened without comment to Jane's retelling of the relative who'd assumed a new identity, Jane couldn't help noticing a growing look of disbelief on Hilda's face as she spoke.

"I think you must be mistaken, my dear," Hilda said, once Jane had finished her tale. "It couldn't have been my husband you're talking about because he had an enormous family, all of whom lived within ten-minutes of each other. It couldn't have been my husband's predecessor at St. Cuthberts, either. He too was a local man, who grew up in the area. My husband's successor after his retirement was our eldest son. I'm afraid that whichever church it was that your relative may have become vicar of, it wasn't St. Cuthberts. Not at the time you're talking about anyway. Are you sure it wasn't St. Marys?" she asked. "They've had some right funny ones there, I can tell you."

Hilda's husband must have been the vicar of the church of St. Cuthberts at the same time as Roz would have been working as a prostitute in the local area. It would almost certainly have been Hilda who would have been running the soup kitchen which Roz had eaten at. The two must have met. She would have been one of the people that had tried to help Roz and women like her. If Hilda was prepared to help women who she knew to be working as prostitutes, and her husband officiate at their marriages, then the couple can't have been judgemental. Nor did she live anywhere near Marlowe, although it was possible she had a relative who did. Jane thought it highly unlikely that Hilda was the letter writer, but if she was, that should be clear in her response to the mention of the letters. If she wasn't, she might have an inkling who was. Jane decided to come clean, making sure she didn't betray anything which might lead to Roz's identity.

"Would it surprise you if I told you that I was really a private detective and what I have just told you wasn't really true?" Jane began.

Hilda daubed biscuit crumbs from her lips with a paper napkin, and said, "I was a vicar's for wife years. No one and nothing surprises me, love, and you being a private detective is a lot more convincing than that last cock and bull story of yours."

"I should have come clean straight away, but I was trying to protect my client," she explained.

Jane produced a copy of part of one of the letters sent to Roz with Roz's name and address blacked out, as was any reference to Marlowe, Greater Flyborough, or the local elections. Before she handed it to Hilda, she said, "I'm trying to find out who sent this to my client. There are many more like this one. To protect my client's confidentiality, I can't let you have too many details, but there is a connection between my client and St. Cuthberts dating to the 1970s. My client has moved on with her life, and no longer leads the type of life she did back then. But, as you will see from these letters, someone doesn't want to let her bury the past. Is there anyone you knew back then, who no longer lives locally, and who might have come across women living as my client did back then, who might be capable of such vindictive behaviour all these years later?" Jane asked, finally passing the letter over to Hilda Lawley.

Hilda read the letter slowly, smiling and nodding to herself as she did so, in a knowing way. When she'd finished, she left it lying in her lap, and said to Jane, "I'm glad your client has been able to rebuild her life. Surprisingly, a lot do, but they have to go to hell and back first. I do know who wrote these letters, and all the others you say were sent. I knew before I started the first sentence, I'm ashamed to say."

CHAPTER SEVENTEEN
The Poison Pen Pal

I

"Henry was Alfred's and my second son," explained Hilda Lawley, after informing Jane she believed the letter writer to be her own son, Henry Lawley. "His elder brother succeeded his father as the vicar of St. Cuthberts. Henry followed his elder brother into the church, only to be told in his first year that he would never progress in the church, and maybe he should consider another career. No official reasons were given for his rejection, other than he was considered unsuitable for advancement. He continued to press for a reason and so finally got an explanation – 'It's the way you interact with your parishioners. We are here to guide and offer help where possible, not act as Lord high executioner, Henry.' – Is what he was told.

"He always was obnoxious," his own mother continued. "He and his brother were like chalk and cheese. His father had to ban him from the soup kitchen in the end, because he kept telling the girls they were going to burn in hell. He runs a printing press in Marlowe-on-the-Water. I don't have his number, I'm afraid. We don't talk any more. I'm sure you can get it from directory enquiries."

Well, well, well, Jane thought to herself. He ran a printing press in Marlowe-on-the-Water. It made sense.

As there wasn't enough time for Jane to travel from Greater Flyborough to Marlowe that day, she decided to return home to Failsham. Whilst still on the train she obtained Henry Lawley's number from directory enquiries and telephoned him. His wife answered the phone. Jane asked if she could arrange an appointment call on Mr Lawley to discuss some printing she needed to be done.

"I need some business cards prepared for me," Jane explained. "Will he be about tomorrow?"

"He'll be in tomorrow morning, if that's all right?" Mrs Lawley said. "About eleven?"

As soon as she got home, Jane looked through the list of names she'd collected from both the churches at Marlowe-on-the-Water. From the list of names she'd obtained from St. Magdalene's, she realised that Henry Lawson was its choirmaster and from his webpage, that he printed literature for the same local council Roz was running for.

II

Henry Lawley met Jane at his front door. He was a tall man with high cheekbones and a pointed nose.

"Good to meet you," he said, shaking her hand firmly. He spoke very carefully and deliberately and with an accent which suggested an expensive education.

"Likewise," she replied.

"Shall we go round to my studio and we can discuss your needs, and I'll show you my work?" he suggested.

On the way there, Jane said, "I understand you do quite a lot of work for the local council?"

"Quite a lot. For example, I print all the council members' business cards for them."

"Really? So you know everyone on the council?"

"I call each member individually after every election, so I get to know who's who," he replied, leading her towards a white summerhouse with a red roof, red windowsills, and a covered porch on which wooden chairs and a table rested. How enchanting, Jane thought as they approached the little house on wheels.

"My printing press," Henry Lawley explained, opening the door of the summerhouse. "Let me show you some examples of my work, Mrs Hetherington. I'm sure I'll be able to accommodate you."

Jane followed him inside the small building, which he'd converted into a printing press. Henry Lawley's work covered the walls from ceiling to roof. P.C towers and monitors stood next to each other and a large printer noiselessly printed out page after page. Piles of plastic covers and ring binders filled a corner of the office. Jane had no doubt that if she opened one of the cabinet's drawers, she'd find the pale blue paper and matching envelopes, used to compose the letters to Roz.

"My wife tells me you're interested in business cards? Allow me to show you a selection I've printed for other people," he said, holding out the only chair in the room for her. He handed her a ring binder of his work. She made a play of opening it and studying its contents.

"These are the standard sized business cards, but obviously I can make them bigger or smaller as you wish. If you give me an idea of exactly what you want, I can give you an idea as to costs. We could make up a prototype here and now, if you like," he suggested helpfully.

Jane looked at him. It never ceased to amaze her how pleasant the most unpleasant people could make themselves appear to be.

"I don't think that'll be necessary. Maybe you could sit down yourself for a few minutes, Mr Lawley," she said, abruptly.

These remarks clearly confused him, but she was a potential customer and he indulged her by sitting down on the edge of the desk.

"Yes?" he said, an arrogant undertone to his voice, revealing the real Henry Lawson.

Jane opened her handbag and took out the sample letter, she'd shown to Hilda Lawley, and handed it to him.

"I believe it was you who wrote and sent this and the other letters?" she said.

Lawley initially looked shocked.

"How the…?" He jumped to his feet, his face flushed with embarrassment.

"I don't think that's important, do you? I'm going to assume from your reaction that you did."

Lawley stared disdainfully at Jane. It hadn't taken him long to recover his composure, Jane thought, watching him flush with anger and spew forth.

"What of it?" he said, contemptuously.

"Well, for a start, sending such letters is against the law, Mr Lawley. I believe you could be sent to jail for a crime such as this. Then there is the morality…"

"Morality," he interrupted. "You come here to lecture me on morality. Did you lecture that woman on her morality?"

"I haven't come here to lecture anybody."

"That common harlot."

Jane was not going to allow him to continue in this vein, which she could see becoming increasingly unpleasant, and therefore she, in turn, interrupted him.

114

"Mr Lawson, as you very well know, all that was many, many years ago," she said calmly. "Everyone is entitled to a second chance."

He ignored her and continued his rant.

"My wife and I weren't rich, but my wife didn't prostitute herself to send our children to decent schools. We scrimped and saved," he said, overflowing with self-righteous indignation.

Jane didn't know what Henry Lawson meant by his words, and was about to say so, when she remembered what Roz had said to her when they'd first met. There must have been a time, Jane realized, when this man had harassed Roz so much that she'd told him she was on the game only so she could put her kid through private school, and he must have believed her. Maybe he'd driven past her in his car one night, yelling insults at her and threatening her, and she'd yelled this back at him, anything just to get rid of him. This made her wonder whether he'd been kerb crawling. If he had been, she bet his wife didn't know anything about it.

"Is that woman going to suggest to her constituents that they put their teenage daughters on the game, if they want something they can't really afford?"

"Mr Lawley I really don't think this is getting us any further. Nobody is denying what happened in the past, but the reasons for it were, I understand, far more complicated than you would have them be. Not that any of that is relevant now. The point is that it isn't happening any longer, and in the end it is none of our business," she said. "You really must stop sending these letters, or I'll have to call the police."

"None of my business," Lawley shouted.

He ran behind the desk and rummaged around in a draw until he found what he was looking for – one of Roz's campaign fliers. The flyer was dark blue and her name was emblazoned across the front of it in white letters.

"I get this through my letterbox, announcing she wants to represent me. To look after my interests," he said, waving the leaflet at Jane and standing rather too close to her for comfort. "Next I'll have her knocking on my door in person to ask for my vote, and you tell me it's none of my business. That I should be represented by a common, a common, a …" he stopped himself. "I refuse to use the word in your presence." He paused. "Whatever you may think about me, that woman is running for public office and she should have been honest about her background and she hasn't been."

No, but then I rather suspect that neither have you, Jane thought. She knew there was no point trying to reason with someone like Henry Lawley. She could have spent the whole of the next week arguing with him and he would still be as intransigent as ever. Without saying another word, she picked up the letter, put it into her handbag, and quietly stood up and walked out of the summerhouse studio. She gently closed the door behind her. She hadn't reached the back gate, when Lawley caught her up.

"If that woman continues to run for the council, I'll continue sending her letters," he hissed. "Call the police if you want to. By all means do so. I don't mind going to jail for my principles. In fact it would be an honour."

Did he mean it, Jane wondered, or were his words an empty threat, spoken because wanted Roz to withdraw from the race least she recognise him? At that moment, a flustered and concerned Mrs Lawley appeared in the back door. She stared back and forth between her husband and Jane in astonishment, eventually running over to her husband to find out what was going on. Jane nodded once in her direction and stepped through the back gate.

From the town centre, Jane sent Roz a text. 'I'm in Marlowe. I think we should talk. Is there anywhere we can meet?'

'I'm in all day and there's no one else here. I'll give you my address and you can come straight round,' Roz replied immediately.

Less than two hours after meeting the charming Henry Lawley, Jane drank coffee in Roz's front room, while Roz smoked continuously. The ashtray on the coffee table overflowed with cigarette butts, and the house stank of cigarette smoke. Jane couldn't help noticing that even the walls and curtains were permeated with it.

"He's a vicar's son?" Roz said, amazed.

"Apparently," Jane said. "His mother is such a lovely woman. She knew it was her son who had written those letters, before she'd read more than a few words. She said he'd always been, and I quote, 'a sanctimonious little prig,' who got worse and worse as he got older. She even went as far as to say that she didn't know what she and her husband had done to deserve him."

"Poor bloody cow," Roz said. "I remember Hilda alright. She was okay to us girls, she was. I don't remember her son, Henry, though."

"Well, obviously he must have remembered you. Take it as a compliment. You must have made an impression. Now you know his identity, what are you intending to do?"

Roz's answer both surprised, and rather saddened her.

"Skulk away with my tail between my legs, I suppose."

"Really?"

"I know, I know. I was going to face him down, but it's all right saying something and another doing it."

"Are you worried people will still judge you, even after all these years?"

"More than worried, certain of it. Let's face it, no one will ever look at me in the same way again. What about my grand kiddies? What am I meant to say to them? And my hubby and son? It's okay saying you're going to be brave and a trailblazer, but another doing it. Who wants aggro, when it can be avoided? I'm going to drop out of the election and that should be an end of it. Me hubby didn't want me to run anyway. Worried I wouldn't be at home to cook his dinner, no doubt," she joked.

While Jane would admit to being slightly disappointed by Roz's decision, she understood it completely, and had no doubt that she would do the same thing were she in Roz's position. She'd stood up to take her leave, when she remembered something. "I almost forgot," she said, searching through her large shoulder bag. "Here." She held out a copy of the St. Magdalene's church magazine to Roz. "I picked it up in Henry Lawley's office. It has a picture of him in it, if you're interested. I've marked the page for you."

Roz took the magazine from Jane, and opened it at the page Jane had marked for her, by folding down a corner. Roz stared at the picture of Henry Lawley for some time before bursting with laughing. "Yeah, now I remember him. He was one of my regulars."

"That's what I suspected," Jane said. "No wonder he wanted you to drop out, he was terrified you'd recognize him – nothing more virtuous. You've got as much on him, as he has on you now. I doubt you'll hear from him again, whether you run or not. I suspect he may hurriedly stop printing the council's business cards if you win your seat."

"I'm still going to drop out," Roz said. "My hubby wants to move nearer to his sister, I'm going to agree. I'd rather forget my past, not worry I'm going to be reminded of it, by bumping into him in the street."

CHAPTER EIGHTEEN
The History of the Failsham Wool Shop

Jack called into the library on his way back from school. He found two books of interest and took them home. In his room he opened the first: *Well-known County Towns and their Buildings.* According to its index, it had a section on Failsham.

'Probably the oldest parts of Failsham are its market square, where a market has been held without break since at least the mediaeval times, and two buildings found there, a 15th century coach house – the White Lion – – and an old haberdashery shop,' the book's author informed its readers. 'My own investigations have revealed that a haberdashery shop in some form has been in the exact same location for two hundred years. I have even found what I believe to be a reference to Failsham's market square in the Domesday Book, although whatever the origins of these buildings were in existence then, I cannot say.'

The writer, a man from the local area, went on to state:

'There's a haberdashery still trading in the same locale, which I have recently visited. That building probably dates from about 1890, however, from my inspection of it, I would say that part of the rear wall of the building might be mediaeval in its construction, with the remainder of the building having been replaced and added to over the years. It's difficult to be certain without removing centuries of plaster, but if I were to hazard a guess, I'd say it was.'

The author finished with the words,

'Wouldn't it be wonderful, if it was!'

It would, thought Jack. He opened the second book he'd borrowed: *The Diaries of Margaret Jones, Daughter of the Rector of Failsham* and read its narrative. Margaret Jones had been born in 1710, and her diaries first published posthumously by her widower in 1738. The diaries were published in five parts. The first part covered her childhood. From the minute he began reading the diary entries, Jack was gripped, something he couldn't quite believe himself.

Margaret had been born and raised in Failsham, her childhood having been spent in the rectory which existed then. Margaret had been the only daughter of the household, until on her ninth birthday, a girl called Agnes Newmark, described by Margaret as, 'my much loved cousin,' joined the household. Agnes was to live with Margaret's family until her marriage. In her diaries, Margaret described many trips taken to the small haberdashery in the market square of Failsham, with her cousin Agnes, to 'purchase dress materials, ribbons for our hair, bonnets and wool with which to knit blankets for the poor babes of the Parish.'

Jack was disturbed from his reading by Charity knocking on the door to ask if everything was all right.

"I'm reading this." He waved the book at Charity, who stared back with bemusement. Getting Jack to read anything was an achievement. "Local history is fascinating, just don't tell anyone I said so," Jack said.

"Well, I've seen everything now," Charity said, closing the door and leaving him to his book.

Jack read until midnight, when he eventually fell asleep, book in hand and light on. The book was gently removed, and the lights turned off by his sister.

The next morning Jack came across the most interesting passage in the book to date:

'Today, Monday, Seventeen May at eight o'clock in the morning, my darling cousin Agnes, announced her betrothal to Samuel Bailey, the son of the haberdashery shop proprietors. Samuel yesterday attended Agnes's family home to ask her dear papa for his daughter's hand in marriage, to which proposal he readily agreed. There could not be one person on earth more joyful at the happiness of a much loved cousin than I on hearing this news,' Margaret penned.

"Samuel Bailey?" Jack repeated.

He ran downstairs to speak to his sister. He found her in the kitchen and read the passage back to her.

"You don't think our Bailey sisters could be a direct descendant of Agnes do you?" he asked.

"Could well be," Charity said, eating a slice of toast. "Tell you what. I'm going to have to re-hang the cupboard door before it falls off..."

Jack looked over to the kitchen cupboard in question. It had been hanging at an angle for some time, but now no longer opened and closed properly. Jack waited for his sister to inevitably add, '... since Johnny's decided he prefers penguins to us, and I have to do stuff like that myself,' but she didn't. Instead she said, "...you help me with that, and I'll help you check the online census, see what we can come up with."

As it was the weekend, the two spent the rest of the day reading through online census after online census, sustained by plates of bacon sandwiches, with lashings of brown sauce. Every decade, they came across at least one Bailey living at the wool shop. As the centuries passed, the size of the families living at the wool shop decreased, and the mention of any servants slowly vanished, but one surname kept cropping up – the surname of Bailey.

"There's been a Bailey running some sort of haberdashery in Failsham's market square for centuries," Charity said, deciding to chart the family's history. She wiped the kitchen's whiteboard clear of its 'to-do' list, and with a black marker pen, wrote down the names of the family members they had discovered so far. She began with Agnes and Samuel Bailey, listed their children below them, and continued with every generation until she reached the end of the line – the three Bailey sisters. An earlier census mentioned a brother, but no further reference could be found of him after he would have turned twenty-one and Charity and Jack decided he must have moved away or died.

"So, Agnes must have been the great, great, great, great, great…" Charity said, tapping each name with her marker pen in turn as she counted. She hesitated. She'd lost count and had to begin again.

"Go on," Jack teased her.

"Great, about twenty times, grandmother of the sisters. Do the Bailey sisters know about this?"

"Not as far as I know," Jack said.

"You need to get this written up as soon as possible, Jack. They'll be fascinated to learn this."

Jack returned to his room to type up his project on his laptop.

'The wool shop in the market square of Failsham may have existed, in some form, since mediaeval times. I discovered this myself whilst researching its history. Although the mediaeval shop isn't the same wool shop where you and I can go and purchase our wool today, part of that ancient building may indeed include the back wall of the very same wool shop which is the subject of this project. The writer will admit to being surprised at how interesting he found the research, and what a fascinating history the wool shop turned out to have. In the following pages, I will attempt to share with you some of that history, including lots of tales of Failsham, its wool shop, and the goings-on of its townspeople, through the years. (In some cases, I have changed the names of those concerned.)

On my Page, I will be posting a visual guided tour of the wool shop, over which I have narrated more of the shop's history and full transcripts of my interviews with the sisters, including more humourous tales.'

Jack felt it incumbent upon himself to mention the proposed redevelopment. He therefore ended his project with the words: 'Many of you will already be aware that the local authority wishes to redevelop the market square, believing it will bring a new lease of life to Failsham town centre. The proposed redevelopment may well do that, but it will also mean the end of the wool shop, something which this young resident will be sorry to see.'

He pressed Send and just met the deadline.

CHAPTER NINETEEN
May the Best Man Win

I

When Felix woke up on Sunday morning, he did so quite refreshed. He wasn't overly concerned about the Bailey sisters objections to the proposed demolition of the wool shop. The shop and the properties on either side of it were in an appalling state of repair. Levelling them to the ground was the best thing for the town, and he was sure the majority of the townsfolk agreed with him there. He didn't really believe there was anything the sisters could do to derail the redevelopment, and their threats to do so, a storm in a teacup. He hadn't wanted to upset them, but still believed a move to somewhere else to be in their best interests, and remain confident they would eventually come around to the idea.

He began his day by escorting Mirabella to church, where he watched her give the morning Holy Communion service, nodding throughout her rousing sermon on the foolishness of vanity. Afterwards, he joined Mirabella at the church entrance to thank the congregation for their kind attendance that morning, as they filed out of church.

Felix Dawson-Jones was not a man to bear a grudge, and therefore, even though one of the Bailey sisters had tried to tip a jug of water over him only days earlier, when it was their turn to leave the church, he said cheerily, "Good morning, ladies. The day finds you well, I hope? The weather is turning, it will be spring soon."

He wasn't particularly downhearted when they ignored him and turned to speak to his wife instead. "We'll see you this afternoon, Rector," Lettice said, on behalf of her sisters.

He shrugged it off, when they pointedly did not say goodbye to him.

Semi-retirement rather agreed with Felix Dawson-Jones. His time was his own to do with as he chose, and with church over, the day was now his. On their way to church that morning Mirabella had said, "My various parish duties shouldn't take up too much time and as the Reverend is performing Evensong, why don't I cook us up a rare roast beef for this evening?"

He climbed into his car wearing a big smile, knowing that after an afternoon of golf, followed by a few clubhouse beers, a roast dinner would be waiting for him when he got home.

II

"I'm home," he cried, stepping through his backdoor. He deposited his golf clubs in the utility room and appeared in the kitchen. There weren't any pans bubbling on the hob. The oven was stone cold and he could not smell anything remotely like his dinner. He opened the oven door. It was empty. At that moment, his son, Miles, walked into the room.

"Where is your mother?" he demanded, his arms folded, a look of fury growing on his face, "and, almost as importantly, where is my dinner?"

Miles shrugged. "Dunno. I'm going out for pizza in town. See yer."

As his son walked out of the kitchen, his wife walked into it.

"How was your day?" she asked him.

"Clearly not as busy as yours," he said, opening the empty oven.

"Did you not eat at your club?"

"I barely ate a morsel…" said Felix, who had eaten a lunch of venison pie with game chips, "…not wishing to ruin my appetite for the evening roast beef, I believed I was to enjoy with my family, 'as the Rev is performing Evensong,'" he quoted.

"I confess to having forgotten all about it. The beef is still in the freezer. I got tied up with things."

"What things?"

"Well, you might as well know. The old ladies have asked me to spearhead their campaign to prevent the closure of their shop. They said I was the best person for the job."

"Please don't tell me you said yes?"

"I've always liked the old ladies."

"I like them, but the redevelopment is in Failsham's interest, my dear."

"But not necessarily in theirs. Anyway I said I would," Mirabella said crisply.

"What?"

"You may have to look after yourself for a bit. The campaign may take up a lot of my time."

"What does, look after myself for a bit, mean?"

"Well for a start it means, you'll need to get your own dinner from now on."

"Get my own dinner?" Since the moment of his birth, Felix Dawson-Jones had not once prepared a single morsel of food for himself. One of the reasons he'd fallen in love with Mirabella was because she was such a good cook.

127

"I'll have a great deal to do. Penny and I have already made a start," she said of their granddaughter, who, along with Penny's mother, Susannah, lived with Felix and Mirabella.

"We've prepared some posters," Mirabella continued. "Here let me show them to you. You can tell me what you think." She called out to Penny to bring her one of the posters, and the child quickly ran into the room holding one. "If I show them to you now, you won't crash the car when you see them everywhere," Mirabella said, unrolling the poster to reveal a photograph of the wool shop, above the words:

'Save Our Wool shop

Our lovely old wool shop is threatened with demolition. Would you rather have a traditional old business run from a traditional old building, or a modern industrial unit in your market square?

Please write to lobby the local council or post any comments on our social networking site: failshamwoolshop@myksau.com.'

"The old ladies have their own social networking site?" Felix said.

"They will soon," his wife said. "Penny and I are going to put these posters up tomorrow, aren't we Penny?" The girl nodded eagerly. "We'll plaster the wool shop windows with them, naturally. We'll see how many shopkeepers and others we can persuade to display them. I may also prepare fliers in a similar form to put through people's letterboxes," she mused. "I promised I'd pen a handwritten letter to the council, asking them to remember they are dealing with three very elderly ladies, and to please give every consideration possible to the redevelopment proceeding without the need to demolish the wool shop."

"How can we proceed without demolishing the shop?" her husband demanded. "It's in the middle of the site!"

Mirabella ignored him.

"I may host a fund-raising evening. If the ladies refuse to move, I may need to take them food."

"Whilst your own husband starves?"

"I don't think either of us is in danger of imminent starvation just yet," she replied, patting his large stomach. "I'll probably be asked to give interviews to give the other side of the story."

Felix spun around in a complete circle and said furiously, "There isn't another side! Not one that's rational. The decision was one taken by the whole council unanimously. It has overwhelming public support. Starving me into submission won't help, and for your information, I am perfectly capable of looking after myself. I can always make myself a salad."

"Salad? You?"

She and Penny could only laugh.

"Yes – salad. As you have already pointed out, I could do with losing some weight." He patted his stomach. "You fight for the old ladies cause, if you wish. I will fight for the town, and may the best man win," he said, wagging his finger at her. "Now if you don't mind, I'm going to chop wood."

Once in the back garden, he removed his jacket and laid it down on the garden bench. He chose a block of wood and rested it on top of the chopping block. He raised the axe above his head and brought it down on the log. It broke neatly in half. He picked up the two pieces and hurled them back on to the woodpile. The second log didn't break so easily, and it took him a few attempts, with the log stuck firmly on to the blade, to split it down the middle.

However much this wood-chopping helped him vent his frustration at a world which seemed to be turning against him, his rumbling stomach reminded him of his predicament – Felix Dawson-Jones hated salad, but not as much as he hated old-fashioned wool shops owned by stubborn spinsters.

CHAPTER TWENTY
The Case of the Philandering Husband

Jane couldn't believe it was Sunday already. She didn't know where the week had gone. Her fridge was almost empty and she was running out of clean clothes to wear, yet there she was, walking into Orla Wilson's Sunday school class, about to start on a new case.

The class had already begun by the time Jane arrived. About twenty children, ranging in age from four to ten, sat on the ground facing a stage at the far end of the hall, where a woman (whom Jane took to be Orla Wilson) stood. The children became quite excited upon finding that they had been joined by a newcomer and began to whisper amongst themselves, turning around to stare at Jane. One little girl smiled sweetly at her and she smiled back. Up on stage, Orla clapped her hands.

"Face the front, children," she barked.

The children fell silent and turned around to face Orla, who was dressed in a 1980's style Laura Ashley floral print dress, buttoned-up to her neck with long sleeves. Despite it only being February she wore open-toed leather sandals. A hair band held her fringe away from her face. She glanced once at Jane, before turning her attention back to the children.

"Now children, on the count of three, I want you to look through the toy box and find the animals the Bible tells us were in Noah's Ark. I want them in rows, ready to board the Ark, two by two."

The children stirred expectantly, but remained in their places, as Orla counted out, "One, two… wait for the count of three, boy," she ordered one lad, who was shyly shuffling forward on his bottom. The other children laughed. "Three," Orla shouted. The children instantly jumped to their feet and swarmed over and up onto the stage. Some used the small row of wooden steps at the far edge of the stage to reach it, while others hoisted themselves straight up onto it from the floor. Once there, they all ran over to a large wooden box in the middle of the stage and surrounded it. The children opened it, and noisily pulled out various wooden animals, which soon lay scattered on the floor. Orla left the children rummaging through the box, and climbed down the stairs slowly and deliberately. Jane walked forward to meet her and they shook hands.

"Jane Hetherington," Jane said.

"Orla Wilson," Orla replied.

Orla was in her early to mid twenties. Her long, straight brown hair needed washing, and she wasn't wearing any make-up.

They moved to sit at the back of the hall. On the stage, the children were still busy removing small painted animals from the toy box with shouts of: "Got one." "I've got a giraffe." "Were there any elephants in the Ark?" "If there are elephants now, stupid, there must have been elephants in the Ark."

"I'm so glad you received my letter, Mrs Hetherington," Orla said. "You never know with the post these days and I cannot abide e-mail. I do not like it one bit. I believe it to be ungodly. We do not have a computer at home."

What an odd woman, Jane thought, clinging on to a world that was over before she was born. Without the internet, Jane would be lost. She wouldn't even have a business.

"How can I help you, Mrs Wilson?"

"I would like you to follow my husband, Peter," Orla said.

Ah? So that's it, Jane thought. It's going to be a case of the philandering husband.

"Please go on," Jane said.

"My husband is twenty-seven years my senior. He was a committed bachelor before he met me. Nobody in our church could believe it when we announced our engagement. He'd convinced everyone that he would never marry. But, as I said at the time, he just needed to find the right woman, that's all." She laughed at this. "We've been married three years and have a two-year-old son and I've just discovered I'm expecting again."

"Congratulations," Jane said, uncertain whether congratulations were actually called for in the circumstances. The conversation was interrupted by a small boy running up to them, holding a plastic dinosaur in his hand. A slightly older boy followed the second. Both were breathless.

"I told him, there weren't any dinosaurs on the Ark because they were too big and heavy and the Ark would have sunk if they'd got on board, so Noah told them to go away and that's why there aren't any dinosaurs left," the eldest boy said, almost without inhaling. "But he won't believe me."

"Are there any dinosaurs on earth, Beade Junior?"

The boy with the plastic dinosaur in his hand ruefully shook his head.

"No, there aren't. Your brother is correct in what he says. Now put that dinosaur back in the toy box and choose another animal. One that was on the Ark."

133

Jane stared at Orla, amazed at what she had just heard her tell the boys.

"Can I pick a fly?" the boy asked. "I saw a dead one in the bottom of the toy box."

"Only if you can find a lady fly for it," Orla said, without a hint of irony.

The two boys ran back to the stage.

"Ever since we first married, my husband has spent some weeks at home and some weeks away," Orla explained. "He's a travelling salesman. I accept the absences, as I accept that some weeks he earns more money than others. We've never had a great deal of money, but recently there has been less than normal, even though he's been working away from home for longer periods. I don't really know how much he earns or where he works. If I need to call him, I call him on his mobile phone and he calls me back when it suits him. I don't really like mobile phones either, but Peter insists we had one because of his absences. I accept without question that it is my role to look after the home and his, the finances. I believe that's how things should be between a husband and wife, Mrs Hetherington. Things would be better in this world if everyone lived the way we do. I really do believe that."

Jane listened to this with some bemusement. Orla was clearly born out of her time, although Jane was uncertain what time Orla should have been born into. Jane couldn't help thinking that even the 1880s might have been too progressive for Orla. It was as though the woman had taken a vow to avoid the modern world.

"Why exactly do you require my services, Mrs Wilson?"

Orla fidgeted with the hem of her dress, crinkling it up in her hand, only to let it go again, smooth it out, before closing her fist around it and crinkling it up again. "Peter brought home so little money last month that I had to ask my parents to help out. Every month he seems to bring home less and less. When I asked him why he was working harder, but we had less money, he shrugged and turned his pockets out, and said, 'I give you all I have. At that moment I don't have much to give you, but that will change, I promise.' God forgive me, but I'm growing suspicious that all he tells me is the truth, Mrs Hetherington," she said, avoiding eye contact. "I'm not sure how I can articulate my suspicions without it sounding as though I am a bad person, which you can tell I am not."

Jane felt enormously sorry for Orla. This was clearly a difficult conversation for her. What a terrible position she was in. Her true-felt religious convictions must have made it all the harder for her.

"You don't need to spell it out, Mrs Wilson," Jane said, attempting to sound reassuring. "I understand how difficult this is for you. You suspect your husband is having an affair, and that is the real reason he is away from home so often, and why there is so little money. You want me to trail him discreetly and find out if this is true?"

Almost immediately, Jane knew she'd said the wrong thing. Orla put her hand over her mouth and stood up. She was red in the face. She looked as though she wanted to explode in anger, but the presence of the children stopped her. She sat down again.

"Adultery is a sin, Mrs Hetherington," she said, still far from composed. "My husband is a man of God. My husband would not commit a mortal sin."

"I'm most terribly sorry if I've offended you in the least," Jane said. "I apologise if I've jumped to the wrong conclusion, but I'm a private detective and following spouses suspected of adultery is the bread and butter of my profession."

"Yes, you must come across a lot of ungodly people in your profession," Orla said, giving Jane a rather disdainful look. "What I suspect my husband of isn't adultery. I don't suspect him of anything more than of trying to shield me. I believe he may have lost his job and has not been able to tell me this. He is such a good man; he wouldn't hurt me or our child for anything in the world. He just wants to protect us from the evil in the world more than anything else, and that includes worry."

"I see. You think he's pretending he still has his job, while he looks for another one."

Orla nodded vigorously.

"I sincerely do," she said. "The poor man must be worried sick, particularly as I am expecting again. 'You mustn't worry Orla,' he'll be thinking. 'You mustn't upset her by telling her you've lost your job. You will get another job soon enough,' he'll be saying to himself. But jobs aren't that easy to come by at his age. If I ask him directly, I know he will only try and protect me, by not telling me the truth. Please follow him for me. When I am able to prove to him that I know the truth, and that I am strong enough to deal with it, only then will we be able to talk our problems through."

"I'll do everything I can to establish the truth," Jane said.

She parted from Orla with another apology on her behalf, a photograph of Peter Wilson, his car registration number and a niggling feeling that she was going to live to regret taking this case on – a feeling which grew stronger and stronger as she walked to her car. Whilst Orla's explanation of her husband's absences, and their money problems, were a possibility, there were other explanations, far less honourable and frankly more likely. Jane didn't really care to be the person who might have to tell Orla something which might cast her husband in a less than gallant light, if that turned out to be the case. However she'd promised to help Orla, and therefore she would.

CHAPTER TWENTY-ONE
Peter Wilson

Jane parked on the opposite side of the street from the terraced house which was the family home of Orla and Peter Wilson, and watched the couple in the doorway of their house, the front door slightly ajar behind them. Orla glanced briefly in Jane's direction. Satisfied that Jane was in position, she looked back at her husband, just about to leave for one of his business trips, right on cue.

Peter Wilson was quite tall and slim and apart from the greying edges of his hair, it wasn't immediately obvious that he was considerably older than his wife. He held their toddler in his arms. Jane watched Peter pass the toddler back to his mother and kiss his wife and child goodbye. From the family's rusty red Ford Escort he waved his family goodbye and moved off. Orla glanced in Jane's direction again. Jane nodded and drove after him, while Orla carried her child back indoors and shut the front door behind her.

Jane ensured there was always a car between her car and Peter Wilson's Escort. Following him through residential streets was quite easy due to the speed limit. Eventually Peter turned onto the dual carriageway. Jane, who had earlier studied a map of the area, suspected he would do this. She knew the town's dualled ring-road led straight to the motorway and this, she assumed, was where they were now headed.

The two cars travelled in a convoy, moved steadily along the dual carriageway, until Peter suddenly pulled across the road and into the right-hand lane where he accelerated. Jane followed him. They were now going alarmingly fast, capped only by the density of traffic, which Jane suspected was forcing Peter to drive a lot slower than he wished to. This was confirmed when a car in front of him stubbornly refused to exceed eighty miles an hour, causing Peter to flash his lights at the driver and honk his horn.

At junction eight, without warning, Peter pulled back across two rows of traffic and exited the dual carriageway. Jane followed him. The speed at which he'd pulled across the traffic had left her so little time to act that had he not been some way ahead of her, she would have missed the turning completely. They were now on the motorway – she ten cars behind – watching him roar along the outer lane, getting further and further away from her, despite her being only minutes behind him. This man must be doing one hundred miles an hour, Jane thought. She would not allow herself to drive at this speed and it wasn't long before she'd lost sight of his car. Damn! Damn! Damn! she said out loud.

She continued to drive along the motorway for an hour, hoping to see his car either up ahead, or parked by a roadside restaurant, but she didn't. She'd have to call Orla and tell her what had happened, promising to try again. She pulled into a lay-by and telephoned Orla from there. She began to explain what had just happened, but found herself interrupted.

"He was driving at what speed?"

"Rather too fast for me to be able to find out," Jane replied.

"My husband does not drive fast," Orla said angrily. "He would never exceed the speed limit. He's a conscientious, law-abiding family man. You must have followed the wrong car, woman."

"I can assure you I…" Jane said, only to find herself interrupted again.

"You were following the wrong car, that's all there is to it. I'll let you know when he's next away, you can have another go. Only next time, make sure you follow the right car, woman," Orla said, abruptly ending the call at her end.

Orla had sounded so insistent, that for a moment, Jane did wonder if she had indeed been following the wrong car. Of course she hadn't, she told herself. The car was quite distinctive. It had one of those irritating 'Baby on Board' signs hanging in the back window, and was seemingly held together by black duck tape, which covered both rear wheel arches. Until it had reached the motorway, Jane had not let it out of her sight. There was obviously something a bit Jekyll and Hyde about Peter Wilson and this whole case. Contrary to what Orla Wilson believed, Jane was now certain there was nothing innocent about Peter Wilson's excursions at all. From the wheel of her car, she mimicked Orla. "I don't have to put up with your rudeness, woman, but my interest has been aroused and I am intrigued to know what is going on, sufficiently intrigued to continue the chase."

CHAPTER TWENTY-TWO
Opportunity Knocks

I

Jane returned home to find messages left on both her landline number and mobile (which she always kept switched off in the car) from James Haley asking if she could call him back. She did so immediately.

"Fonebies have verified the sketches," he said, the excitement clear in his voice. "They're authentically Jasper August and they date to the right time. We've even found a couple of his thumbprints on them! I'm ecstatic. I hope you are too. We intend to announce the discovery to the media tomorrow morning."

"Please remember, I'd rather have my name left out of things if there's going to be any publicity," Jane reminded him.

"There will be some publicity, but not as much as if we'd found a long-lost portrait. Don't worry – I'll make sure you're not mentioned by name."

"In that case, I'm more than happy to sell you my sketches for the sum we agreed, Mr Haley."

The minute she came off the phone from James Haley, she telephoned Graham Burslem.

"Told you it was genuine," he said.

The money would be in her account by the end of the day, she explained and once there, she'd deduct her bill and expenses and arrange for the balance to be sent straight through to his bank account as agreed.

"Thank you my dear," he said. "I don't know what I would have done without you."

She came off the phone to discover Orla Wilson had called when she'd been on the phone to Graham

Burslem. Jane listened to a blunt message informing her that Peter Wilson was going away again the very next day, and could Jane follow him, and this time could she try to follow the right car.

"I'll try," Jane said meekly, replacing the receiver.

Having checked her answer phone messages, she decided to check her e-mails. She found one from her neighbour, Charity, which was unusual. Attached to the brief message – 'Hasn't the boy done good!' – were two attachments. The first featured Jack (captured on a mobile phone) standing at the front of his classroom next to his teacher.

"All of the projects handed in were of a very high standard and congratulations to all of you, you have clearly all worked very hard at this project," the teacher said. "However, I must pick Jack out for the highest praise. I couldn't put your project about the wool shop down Jack, from the minute I began reading it. You have literally brought to life a building I thought was nothing more than a musty old shop, and I can't wait to watch the virtual reality tour of the shop or better still, pay a visit to the shop myself."

Jack beamed. The camera scanned the room. Some of Jack's classmates clapped, whilst others groaned and pretended to make themselves sick. One even lobbed a paper ball in Jack's direction. The camera zoomed in on a young girl sitting at the back of the classroom. She smiled shyly at Jack, who smiled back. Who's this? Jane wondered.

The second attachment contained Jack's project. Jane printed it out and settled down to read it from the comfort of her living room.

As she read on, a possible way to help the Bailey sisters occurred to her. She called Jack to run it by him.

"Jack your project's fantastic," she said. "You've unearthed so much. Would you mind if I forwarded it on to the local media? It's the kind of story they'd love."

"You think?"

"Absolutely."

"Will I be famous?"

"Maybe for fifteen minutes."

Jane rang up the local news' desk and spoke to a young freelance reporter called Lili Alsop, who she told all about Jack's project and his discoveries about the wool shop. "I personally found the whole thing quite poignant, particularly as the wool shop is facing demolition," Jane said. "Please allow me to e-mail it to you."

II

A short while later, Jack returned home from football practice to hear Charity say,

"He's just this minute got back. I'll have him there in thirty minutes."

"Go upstairs and have a shower," she ordered immediately she'd replaced the receiver. "And wash your hair."

"Why should I?" he argued.

"Because some journalist's on her way to the wool shop as we speak to interview the Bailey sisters about how old the wool shop really is. She wants you to be there as well because you discovered everything."

"But why do I have to wash my hair?" he complained.

143

"Because I don't want people to think you're being dragged up, that's why," Charity barked at him, snatching one of his newly washed shirts from the top of the ironing pile and setting up the ironing board.

CHAPTER TWENTY-THREE
National Treasures

I

The interview took place in the wool shop's tiny parlour room. Jack took his place next to the sisters on the Chesterton, his freshly washed hair neatly combed back, and sporting a crisply ironed white shirt.

"Had you any idea that your little wool shop was one of the oldest of its kind in the country, possibly the oldest?" Lili asked the sisters.

"We had no idea, did we girls?" Dotty said. "Until young Jack told us."

"Please share your part in this with us, Jack?" Lili asked.

"It was just a school project, to start with. I wasn't going to do more than I had to, you know, but the more I learned about the shop and how old it was, the more I wanted to learn about it. I think there's a whole lot more still to learn."

"Are you really sure that our shop is the oldest?" Nellie asked.

"I checked with the Guinness book of records and they don't know of one older," Lili said.

"Oh, we don't know about that, do we girls?" Lettice said. "There may be another one somewhere."

"Well, I'm sure it won't have been run by the same family for four centuries," the young reporter said.

Lili finished her interview by moving the group outside to the market square. She positioned the sisters and Jack on either side of her, and framed the wool shop in the picture behind them. "Such a shame this lovely old shop with such a history is to be lost to redevelopment," she said to the camera, "but I suppose that's progress."

Gene Ward, the executive producer of the country's most popular breakfast television show - Top of the Morning to You TV, known throughout the country as TMTV – watched Lili's interview with the sisters on the regional news programme. He liked what he saw and telephoned the shows' producer to gauge the viewer's response to the interview. He liked what he heard.

"We've been deluged with calls and e-mails about those old ladies," was the reply, "mostly along the lines of the old dears and that shop of theirs, being national treasures which should be preserved. That kid's site's getting hundreds of hits apparently. You really should go national on this one. Those three are tailor-made for breakfast TV."

Gene Ward arrived at the wool shop later the same evening. The sisters cautiously opened its door and lined up, shoulder by shoulder, their arms folded as though prepared for an invasion. He smiled at them, they glowered back at him.

"Who are you? Have you come to knock our house down?" Nellie demanded.

"If you have, it will be over our dead bodies," Lettice said.

"On the contrary. I'd like nothing more than to help you save your wool shop. I've come to ask to you to appear on breakfast TV tomorrow morning, and give

146

your side of the story. Could I come in?" he asked. "It's rather cold out here and it's beginning to drizzle."

The sisters ignored him and moved away to huddle together some way from the front door. After a few moments of consultation, they returned. "No, you can stay right where you are," Nellie said.

"It's not personal, young man," Dotty said to Gene, who was approaching sixty. "It's just that the last time we invited someone into our home, he told us he was going to knock it down."

"I want to save your home. Please hear me out."

They listened patiently as he explained who he was and why he was there. "If you agree to appear on our TV show, millions of people will hear your story."

Once again the sisters left him where he was to huddle together. They returned to tell him they were reluctant to travel to London, and leave their shop unattended, even for one night.

"We might come back and discover they've knocked our home down," Lettice said.

"We'll post a local TV crew outside with a camera, to make sure they can't," Gene promised, impatient to be on his way. It was growing late and raining quite heavily. He didn't have an umbrella and was getting wetter and wetter, something which seemed to leave the sisters unmoved. Again, they left him to talk the proposal over amongst themselves. They returned after about five minutes.

"We accept," Dotty said on behalf of her sisters. "But only because we don't open the shop on Monday. If it had been any other day of the week, we would have had to say no, because we all have to be here to open the shop up."

The rain was literally running down that Gene's back and dripping off his nose. His clothes were drenched through, and his glasses so covered in water he could hardly see any of the sisters. He took them off and dried them on the inside of his jacket, and put them back on. "Great," he said, somewhat through clenched teeth. This indomitable spirit of theirs would undoubtedly go down well with his viewers, he knew, but all it was doing for him right now was causing him to catch pneumonia. "If you don't mind, I'll wait in the car while you pack what you need. It's a little wet out here."

"Never mind that, young man," Lettice said sternly. "Where is that camera crew you promised to guard our property? We're not going until it's here."

"I'll call them right now," he promised.

While the Bailey sisters went to pack, Gene Ward telephoned a freelance cameraman he knew lived nearby, and asked if he would turn up with his camera and sit outside the shop. "Just until I get them into the car, and on their way to London. I'll pay you for an evening's work."

"My sisters and I haven't been to London since 1937," Nellie said, the last of the three old ladies to get into the back of the car. "Do you imagine it's changed much?" she asked Gene, who held open the door.

"I think the least we can do is arrange a tour for you afterwards," Gene promised. He closed the back door and walked back to the driver's seat.

"Do you think you could arrange for us to meet the Queen perhaps?" Dotty enquired. "We would so like to meet her, wouldn't we girls?"

148

"If you're a big hit tomorrow morning and having met you, I'm sure you will be, there'll be nothing you won't be able to do," he said.

CHAPTER TWENTY-FOUR
10 Upper Alan Street, Sheffield

I

Jane had been on Peter Wilson's tail for less than thirty minutes and so far the journey was a familiar one.

The 'Baby on Board' sign bobbed up and down on the back window, the same piece of black duck tape hung off the rear left-hand wheel shaft flapping furiously in the wind, and already touching eighty miles an hour and accelerating, the car had just cut across two lanes of motorway traffic to speed along the right-hand carriageway, with Jane wondering how she was going to keep up.

Just as they passed under a bridge, Peter suddenly reduced his speed and pulled into the inside lane. Jane attempted to do likewise, but she was slightly too slow and ended up driving past the speed trap Peter Wilson had obviously seen and slowed down to avoid. She passed it at seventy-six miles an hour and quickly found herself flagged down. Forced to pull over by the roadside, she could only watch Peter Wilson race away from her. Dammit, she thought, rolling down the car window to the young police officer stood there, breathalyser in hand.

II

The next day, Jane met Ant Dillard in the cafeteria of the Magistrates' Court for lunch. He literally roared with laughter when Jane told him about her being pulled over and breathalysed.

"I've never been so embarrassed in my life," she said. "Me – a part-time lay magistrate!"

"Our fellow magistrates will all find this very amusing," he said, chuckling to himself. "They all hold you in very high esteem, you know. Or rather they did."

"Breathalysed at the roadside. A woman of my age. I just hope no one I know saw me. I managed to reduce my speed down to seventy-six-miles-an-hour, but it was a seventy-mile-an-hour limit. How many points is that? Three or six? And what about my insurance? Will it affect my premiums?"

"You'll have to declare an interest if someone appears before you at the bench for a speeding offence," he reminded her, clearly finding the whole thing highly entertaining.

"This is so infuriating. I still have no idea where Peter Wilson is driving to when he leaves his wife, but I'm certain it's not to job hunt. At this rate, I'll end up losing my driving licence and I'll still be no further to cracking the case." She stared at the uneaten sandwiches she'd bought for her lunch. "I don't know why I bought this, I have no appetite." She pushed her lunch away. "Anything interesting at this morning's session?"

Ant finished off the last few mouthfuls of his burger and French fries and patted his lips with a napkin. "Tramps, thieves and drunks. Who else do we ever see here? Oh, and speeding motorists, of course."

"I'm at my wits end, Ant, I really am. How am I going to find out what Peter Wilson is up to?" she said in despair.

"Fear not, my dear. Leave everything to me. What's his registration number?"

Jane took out her notepad and opened it at the right page. She read out the registration number, which Ant wrote down on a napkin. Armed with this information, he walked over to a couple of young police officers due to give evidence in an overrunning case, drinking coffee at a nearby table. After a brief exchange of words, and a radio conversation between the police station and one of the officers, Ant rejoined Jane.

"His car is registered to an address in Sheffield."

"Sheffield?" Jane repeated.

He handed her a piece of paper, on which the police officers had written down an address.

"10 Upper Alan Street, Sheffield," Jane read. "This is making less and less sense."

Ant, who was enormously proud of his encyclopaedic knowledge of the country's road network, raised his finger. "Oh, but it does. If you were to continue on the motorway until Virginia Waters, then take Junction 12 onto the M25 and stay on it until Junction 21 until you hit the M1, hey presto, you're well on your way to Sheffield. Incidentally, that car's been registered to him at that address for more than ten years."

"Ten years? That's longer than he's been married to Orla. Much longer."

"He's been living at that address for at least that length of time."

"Good heavens. I don't think this is going to turn out to be an open and shut case, do you, Ant?"

"When are your cases ever open and shut, Jane?"

"When indeed? When indeed?" she repeated, deciding she would have lunch after all. There was nothing like a good puzzle to whet the appetite, she always found.

CHAPTER TWENTY-FIVE
Top of the Morning to You

I

To the relief of TMTV's production crew, the Bailey sisters seemed to be quite at ease under the hot TV studio lights. Dan Slack, the show's popular, good-looking, dark haired, Northern Irish anchor, listened attentively, while Lettice Bailey, sandwiched between her sisters on the famous breakfast show sofa, said, "We didn't know the shop was as old as it is, you understand."

"But we did know it was very old, Lettice," Nellie said. "Didn't we, Dotty?"

"We did, Nellie," Dotty said.

"The shop isn't the same as it was when Agnes and Samuel Bailey lived there, of course," Nellie Bailey pointed out. "That was a long time ago. We have running water, gas and electricity," she said proudly. "They wouldn't have had anything like that in those days."

"And thanks to a very nice man from the council, we've had an inside toilet for the last fifteen years," Dotty said.

"It's extraordinary that you still sell wool, as you have done every day for, well, seventy years now," Dan said, in his soft Northern Irish brogue.

"We still enjoy it," Dotty explained. "We love talking to people you see. We learn all sorts of things about people. Things their nearest and dearest don't know about them."

"We once helped a woman leave her cruel husband," Lettice said. "Dotty distracted him in the street outside the shop and kept him talking on the subject of the government of the day, while Nellie and I helped her flee out of the back door. Nellie drove her to the station herself, even though she'd only ever been behind the wheel of a car twice before."

"And never since," Nellie herself said. "It wasn't that difficult, although it did stall more than once."

"It wasn't even her car. We've never had a car," Dotty said.

"It belonged to the squire. He'd parked it outside the shop. I helped myself to it. I left it at the station and walked back. No one ever knew who took that car," Nellie finished her story.

"Have there been any other interesting people you've met over the years?" Dan asked.

"We once served the Prince of Wales's chauffeur," Dotty said. "Not the current one, of course."

"We've never met him," Lettice said. "Or the Prince of Wales."

"Nellie was once proposed to by a customer in the shop, or was that me?" Dotty said. "It was all so long ago now I can't rightly remember who the subject of the proposal was. He got down on bended knee though, and I remember a bouquet of flowers."

"One customer once bought every ball of wool in the shop and the needles. I can't imagine what for," Nellie said. "We couldn't take any more orders until we'd restocked."

"Trade isn't what it once was," Lettice admitted. "But we do so love our wool shop and our customers. At our age, we do think we should be allowed to live out our days doing what we love to do, if we wish to do so."

"I couldn't agree more. Now tell me ladies, are you enjoying the attention all this is bringing you?"

The ladies looked at each other. "Well we didn't to begin with," Nellie said," but now we're beginning to rather enjoy it, aren't we girls?"

"Everyone is in such a hurry these days," Dotty said. "At our age it's difficult to keep up, but since this has happened, people have been in touch from all over the world and we do so love talking to people, particularly the young people, and they do seem to like talking to us."

"We don't feel as though the modern age has left us behind anymore," Lettice said. "We suddenly feel quite in tune with it. Do you see?"

"I'm sure our viewers will have a lot to say on the subject of your wool shop," Dan said. "Now, please tell the viewers, where did you get that unusual name from Lettice?"

"It was my dear Mama's name and her Mama's name before her. It's a family tradition. I'm the eldest you see. I'm ninety next birthday, if I make it."

"I'm sure you'll all be here for many a year to come," Dan said, "and from all of us here on Breakfast TV, I hope and pray that your shop will be as well, with you still in it. Please put aside some of your best wool for my dear old Ma, will you?"

As the camera pulled away from the three sisters, and closed in on Dan Slack, Nellie's voice could be heard saying,

"Are you married young man? You're very dashing, isn't he girls?"

II

"Makes our little poster campaign seem a bit tame, doesn't it, Penny?" Mirabella said in the rectory's kitchen, TMTV playing in the background.

"Everyone will be on their side," Felix said, in exasperation. "We'll have flying pickets outside that shop before we know it."

"Pickets? Why didn't we think of that, Penny?" her grandmother asked.

While her grandmother clapped and chanted, "Keep our wool shop open! Keep our wool shop open!" Penny walked around the room, pretending to hold up a placard.

Felix could only slap his forehead with his hand, when Dan Slack read out a text from a TMTV viewer.

'The council should let the old ladies live out their days in their home if they want to. For heaven's sake, that market square of theirs, or whatever it is they wish to bulldoze, has survived up to now. Where's the harm in leaving things as they are for a few more years?'

"That pretty much sums up the sentiments we're receiving on this one," Dan said.

Felix had seen enough. He switched the TV off. Millions of people watched TMTV live, and many more watched it online, sometimes over and over again. He knew what was going to happen. The ladies wouldn't be through the door of their wool shop before they were offered the chance to sell their story to a national paper. Anyone who had not yet heard of them soon would. In no time they would be telling the whole country their side of the story, and no doubt the whole country would take their side.

Felix knew full well if a local authority took on three extremely elderly ladies, then no matter what

157

justification the council had for doing so, no matter how many people supported the redevelopment, the council and its individual members would always be perceived as the villains of the peace. No one would be interested in the reasons why the council wanted to redevelop the market square, he thought bitterly. All anyone would know or care about was that three old ladies were being thrown out of their lifelong home, so it could be bulldozed to the ground. The council would be notorious. He had never thought himself to be a particularly bad person, but he knew that soon he was a going to find himself depicted as someone only marginally above a puppy boiler. At least things couldn't get any worse, he thought to himself.

III

A few hours later, on the other side of the Atlantic, Bart Bartholomew, the presenter of a top-rated US chat show, the Chat Hour, sat in the studio's galley with the show's producer and director watching the sisters appearance on TMTV.

"They got an agent?" Bart said. "If not, think I'll volunteer my services."

"These old gals for real?" the producer asked. "They're to die for."

"We've got to get them on the show," the director said.

CHAPTER TWENTY-SIX
Book of Lies

I

The large red-brick hall-entrance terraced house on the outskirts of town, given as Peter Wilson's Sheffield address, wasn't dissimilar to the house he shared with Orla.

Jane parked across the road from it at seven a.m. and at nine a.m. watched him say his goodbyes to another family. The woman he kissed goodbye on the doorstep of this house, a good deal older than Orla, was dark haired, portly, and the mother to teenage children. One, a girl, started to cry as Peter Wilson, the man Jane supposed to be the girl's father, bid his farewells. The second child, a boy of about fifteen, looked withdrawn and uninterested in the proceedings. He'd grown used to his father's comings and goings. His mother too, judging by the stoical expression on her face. The family accepted this man's absences, as Orla did.

What story did he tell them by way of explanation, she wondered. The same one he told Orla, or another one? Did he carry on him somewhere a book containing the lies told to each woman? Did he refer to it between visits, to ensure he didn't slip up?

She watched Peter get into his car. The 'Baby on Board' sign had been removed, she noticed. He drove away, followed by Jane. Keep your eyes on the car, and your foot on the accelerator, Jane, she told herself. The heavy, slow moving traffic helped her endeavour. After an hour, and still on Peter's tail, she found herself driving around the ring road of a different city – Manchester. Is this man addicted to commuting, she said to herself. As she said it, she had that sinking feeling again. Where was Peter Wilson going? Not another family, surely, she thought, knowing in her heart of hearts, the answer was almost certainly going to be yes.

Peter Wilson's final destination turned out to be a car park behind a small block of newly built flats. Jane pulled in behind him quite certain he wouldn't recognize either her or her car, despite her having followed him all the way from Sheffield. Peter Wilson, she knew, had other things on his mind. She was right. He walked past her car without a glance. He hadn't reached the block of flats, when the door to a ground floor flat was flung wide open and a woman ran out of it. Peter Wilson opened out his arms and the woman almost jumped into them and the couple began a passionate kiss. For heaven's sake, Jane said out loud from behind the wheel of her car. Put him down woman, he's married. And to more than one woman, she said, this time under her breath.

Two children, a girl and a boy of about ten and twelve appeared in the doorway. Were they Peter's children, or the woman's children from a previous marriage, Jane wondered. They watched the scene sullenly. Unnoticed by their mother or Peter Wilson, the boy looked at his sister, put his fingers in his mouth and pretended to make himself sick. Jane would have put their mother's age as lying somewhere between Orla's age, and the age of the woman in Sheffield. In complete contrast to the other women in Peter Wilson's life, this woman was glamorous. She wore a knee-length, brightly patterned silk dress; high-heeled, open-toed sandals and lashings of makeup and jewellery. Jane felt

160

really rather plain by comparison. She was close enough to spot that the third woman in Peter Wilson's life wasn't wearing a wedding ring. Not yet anyway, she thought.

What do these women see in this man, she wondered. She knew he wasn't rich and in truth, he wasn't particularly good looking, but it wasn't her job to speculate. They all had their reasons. She waited until everyone disappeared inside the apartment block, before driving away.

She returned to Sheffield to pay a visit to its City Hall. There, she set about perusing the online electoral register. The register confirmed that the occupants of 10 Upper Alan St., Sheffield, who would be eligible to vote at the next election, were a Peter Jeremiah Wilson, a Samilla Petra Wilson and a Jeremiah Wilson. This meant that the bored youngster, Jane had seen earlier, was at least seventeen.

Jane walked to the room next-door. This contained the microfiched register of births, deaths and marriages. She sat behind a microfiche reader and began studying the marriage register. The marriage of Peter Wilson and Samilla Hazel had taken place seventeen years earlier, on a Saturday afternoon, in this very building. The record revealed that Samilla Wilson's first marriage had been dissolved and that she would now be forty-nine. Peter Wilson was described as being the widower of Winifred Gertrude Wilson, deceased. Oh yes, Jane thought cynically. Nonetheless, she did spend some time searching unsuccessfully for both the marriage certificate of Peter and Winifred Wilson and the death certificate of Winifred Wilson. When she found neither, she gave up the search and returned to her car.

She sat in the car for some time, before she drove off. She was worried. How on earth she was going to tell poor Orla Wilson that the man she idolized had been lying to her since the day she met him? This wasn't the type of news a rational person would receive well, and she didn't consider Orla rational.

II

The next morning, Jane opened up a database containing the names of every person on the U.K.'s unedited electoral register and the phonebook, and typed in the name Winifred Gertrude Wilson. A few Winifred Gertrude Wilson's came up and next to the names, came the age range of the person concerned and the region of the country they lived in. Jane read down the list. One was a very young child (Jane wondered why anyone would choose such an old-fashioned name for such a young child) and two were very old ladies. The last Winifred Gertrude Wilson listed was given as being between fifty and fifty-five. Bingo, thought Jane, immediately calling directory enquiries. She asked to be put through to a Winifred Gertrude Wilson, Brentford, outer London, hoping she wasn't ex-directory.

She wasn't and a youngish-sounding woman answered the phone.

"I wonder if I could speak to a Mrs Winifred Wilson?" Jane asked.

"Can I ask what it's about?"

"I'd like to ask Mrs Wilson if she knows or knew a man called Peter Jeremiah Wilson." Jane had to be direct, if she were to discover anything.

"Mum," the young woman called out. "There's a woman on the phone asking about Dad."

162

What sounded like a scuffle and arguing followed, although as it was in the background, Jane couldn't make the words out. She wondered if the phone was about to be slammed down on her.

"Give me that," she heard someone say. Another woman came to the phone. "Who are you and what do you want?" This woman was older than the first. She was also very angry.

"My name is Mrs Jane Hetherington. Would I be speaking with Winifred Wilson?"

"What's it to you and what do you want with my husband?" Winifred Wilson said.

Jane didn't blame her for being angry and suspicious.

"I'm trying to establish the whereabouts of a Peter Jeremiah Wilson, who I believe you were once married to."

"Worse luck," was the reply.

"I'm a private detective, you see. I've been asked to try and find him by someone."

"He's walked out on some other poor cow has he?"

"Something like that."

"Well, you're looking in the wrong place, love," Winifred said, "that son of a bitch walked out on me and my kid sixteen years ago and we haven't seen hide nor hair of him ever since, so unless you've got some good news, like he's died rich, leaving me everything in his will, then I'd rather you left me and my daughter alone."

"I quite understand, and I apologise for disturbing you and your daughter," Jane said, the conversation over.

A cup of coffee in hand, Jane went to her conservatory where she did her best thinking. She settled herself down and mulled over Winifred Wilson's words. According to Winifred, Peter Wilson had walked out on her sixteen years ago. Yet he would have been 'married' to Samilla by then and living with her in Sheffield, and their son either already born, or Samilla heavily pregnant with him. Well I never, she thought, two wives (that she knew about) and a possible third wife on the horizon. She didn't even want to speculate how many other women there may be in Peter Wilson's life, which she hadn't stumbled across.

How complicated other people seemed to make their lives, she, who liked to keep her life as simple as possible, mused. No wonder the couple were short of money.

She took out a piece of paper and jotted down what she believed was the sequence of events. If Winifred had divorced Peter by the time he married Samilla, then Samilla would be his lawful wife, not Orla. However, it wasn't clear from their conversation, whether Winifred had divorced Peter. All she'd asked was whether Peter had died and left her money. If they had divorced, but hadn't done so until after Peter had married Samilla, but before he'd married Orla, then the marriage to Samilla would be null and void, and Orla the lawful wife.

This, Jane hoped might at least be of some consolation for Orla. It was a big 'if' and anyway, it didn't really detract from the fact that Orla's marriage was a lie.

CHAPTER TWENTY-SEVEN
Five Thousand Friends

From her study window, Mirabella could see clumps of purple crocuses, royal blue dwarf irises and golden narcissus pushing their way through the rectory's lawn and flowerbeds. This transient, beautiful spring scene was always worth the year-long wait it took to see. At the end of the garden, Felix helped the gardener tie conifer branches, bent out of shape by the heavy snowfall, back into place. Mirabella slowly turned her eyes from the garden to those in the room with her – her granddaughter, Penny, and Jack, just as he let out a squeal on discovering the number of messages posted on the wool shop's social networking site.

"They've got nearly five thousand friends already, and lots more asking to be friends," Jack said wistfully. "Wish I had that many. I've been saying yes to everyone, but I think I'm going to have to be more selective. What criteria should I use?"

"You can only be our friend if you cough up some dough for the campaign fund," Mirabella said.

Penny gently hit Jack on the arm, pointed to the computer screen and said, "You."

Jack knew what she meant. So did her grandmother. "Penny's right, Jack," Mirabella said. "The site's become so popular because of the time you've spent posting all those lovely stories of theirs of times past. You should be the campaign manager, not me."

With Penny playing with a doll, Jack and Mirabella read through the messages of support.

'I loved the old ladies' reminiscences,' someone wrote. 'Hope they keep their shop open.'

'It's the same old story. An ancient way of life destroyed overnight by corporate greed.'

'Poor Lettice, losing her fiancé like that.'

'The story about the poor little boy they knew who died of an infection a year before antibiotics were discovered made me cry.'

'Most affecting,' was how one simple blog put it.

'The sisters have nothing to worry about. Knitting isn't dying out because the young people don't do it anymore. Quite the contrary. I'm a student and I knit. So do most of my girlfriends,' one lady posted.

'There's a lot of us still about. I've knitted all my life and my 10-year-old twins have decided to take up knitting, thanks in no small part to hearing all about the wool shop. Where can we buy its wool from?'

"I suppose we could set up a pay point on their website, and sell the wool online?" Jack suggested. "A virtual wool shop, to replace the bricks and mortar one. How's that for a happy ending?"

"Only so long as it doesn't involve all of us spending hours packing up wool to send all over the world," Mirabella warned, hoping as she said it, that her words would not turn out to be prophetic.

CHAPTER TWENTY-EIGHT
Man of God

I

With Peter Wilson in either Sheffield or Manchester, Jane called Orla at home. Orla answered the phone after only two rings.

"Oh, it's you," she said abruptly. "Have you managed to follow the right car yet?"

"Mrs Wilson are you sitting down? Because I'm afraid I have some very unpleasant news to break to you."

Orla listened in silence while Jane spoke. When Jane had finished, Orla said, "Are you telling me, woman, that my husband is a bigamist?"

"I'm afraid that would appear to be the case, yes."

"How dare you? How dare you ring me at my home to tell me my husband isn't my husband and my kid is illegitimate! That is what you're telling me isn't it, woman?" Orla demanded, her voice growing ever shriller.

"It rather depends on the chain of events," Jane said weakly.

"I married my husband in a church, Mrs Hetherington," Orla said.

"That's as may be," Jane tried to explain.

"We married in a church, we met through our church. He sings in the choir, for God's sake! He is a man of God, woman, a man of God! Not a criminal!" Orla shrieked down the phone. "What you are saying is that the man is a miserable sinner and so am I!"

Jane knew this conversation wasn't going to be easy.

"You've obviously been following the wrong man, the whole time woman."

"Mrs Wilson, I can assure you that I followed your husband. I followed the man you told me to. The man I saw kiss you and your children goodbye on the doorstep. The man who is not only father to your children, but to two other children, born to another woman, whom he married when he was still married to someone else, just like he was when he married you. I'm sorry to be the one to tell you this, but you must believe me."

"I don't believe you. You're lying. Why are you doing this to me? Why are you making up such vile lies, woman? Is it because you're old and bitter?"

Jane ignored these comments and tried to keep calm.

"Mrs Wilson, I am not lying. We're going to have to go to the police about this. There are other people involved here. I believe your husband may be about to marry again when he is still married to you and to those other women. He may even have another child by this woman if we don't stop him."

"Go to the police? With lies about my own husband? I am not going to do any such thing and you're not either woman, if you know what's good for you. I will not let you ruin my happiness because you have none left of your own. If what you tell me is true, how then do you explain my husband being at my home with me, at the same time you say you saw him with another woman in another city? I have friends from my church who were here with us, and who will support my story and prove you to be a liar."

Jane could not explain this for the moment, but she knew what she'd seen.

Orla's rant continued. "I can prove it. We went into town in the afternoon. Our friends saw us there. We will be on CCTV. So you see, I know you are lying. I've a good mind to get you closed down!"

While Jane didn't try to interrupt her, she did hold the phone away from her ear to avoid being deafened.

"And don't think I'm going to pay your bill either, woman," Orla screamed, slamming the phone down.

"Well, that went better than I thought it would," Jane said, replacing the receiver.

II

She went straight around to her neighbour's house to repeat the conversation.

"She said what?" Charity said, walking over to join Jane at the kitchen table.

"Think of it from her point of view," Jane said, a mug of tea in hand. "She's a devout Christian, very much in love with her husband, a man she believes shares her principles, then I ring her up and deliver what could best be described as a bombshell."

"After she asked you to follow him," Charity pointed out. "If it was me, I'd follow him myself. Check the story out with my own eyes."

"But, if she did that, she would discover it was true and she doesn't want to believe that, does she?"

At that moment, Jack walked into the kitchen and over to the fridge.

"What are you two talking about?" he wanted to know.

169

"One of Jane's clients won't believe what Jane has found out about her husband," his sister explained.

Jack helped himself to a can of fizzy drink and joined them at the table. "I read somewhere that even when people pay a private detective like Jane to follow their spouse because they think they're cheating on them, and the private detective comes back with photographs and stuff which proves that their husband or wife is cheating on them, the person who paid the detective in the first place, more often than not refuses to believe the evidence."

"I can't believe that, Jack," Charity said.

"Jack is quite right," Jane said. "Apparently that does happen quite a lot. It's something a private detective has to be prepared for. Denial, anger, depression and finally acceptance. Classic defence mechanisms."

"Why have they paid someone to follow their other half, then?" Charity wanted to know.

"For reassurance, not the truth, unless the truth is that their spouse isn't cheating on them." Jane said.

"I thought I was gullible," Charity said. "What I want to know, is what's he living on?"

"I rather presume it's a combination of the state, handouts from friends and relatives, and the women themselves, of course. Orla isn't in paid employment, but the other two probably are. I suspect that's why he's got himself another girlfriend."

"How do you explain him being in two places at the same time? Do you think she made it up to save face, or is she just mad?" Charity clicked her fingers. "I know – she wanted to stop you from going to the police so her name isn't dragged through the mud."

170

"She seemed very sure of her facts, and adamant she could prove it. I'm not sure she made it up. I wonder if there's another explanation," Jane said.

"Yeah, she's mad," Charity said.

"You know the Bailey sisters are off to New York?" Jack said. "All care of the All American Broadcasting Corporation. It's so unfair. No one's invited me and I found everything out."

"The satisfaction of having helped the sisters should be reward enough, Jack," Charity said.

"Well it isn't."

CHAPTER TWENTY-NINE
Fifteen Minutes of Fame

I

Felix drove to the council offices, but couldn't get into the car park due to the number of vehicles parked in it. Forced to park elsewhere, he returned on foot. He knew that in a few days time, a Rolls-Royce driven by a chauffeur wearing a peaked cap, would pull up outside the wool shop to take the Bailey sisters to the airport for the start of their journey to the States. No doubt they'd be feted by the best of New York society, accompanied everywhere by an AABC camera crew.

Felix smiled at the thought of the extravaganza. He even imagined a Vice-President of AABC saying, "I want the old gals treated like royalty. Royalty – you hear. Give 'em the red-carpet treatment. Take 'em everywhere by a chauffeur driven Rolls-Royce, with champagne in the back."

"I think they are all teetotal," one of his assistants might have pointed out.

"Okay, homemade lemonade then."

He could do no more than wish them all the best. They might as well make the most of the fame they were suddenly enjoying, for if not now, when? He hoped they took the opportunity to indulge themselves a little, for up to now, theirs had been a life of abstinence and frugality, and not a little disappointment. Who knows, he thought, they might let their hair down – literally.

As he got closer to the council building, he saw both the head and the deputy head of the council standing at the top of the building's wide flight of stairs, addressing a noisy crowd gathered by the base of the stairs. He wondered what on earth was going on.

As he grew closer he realised the noisy crowd were journalists who, as Felix grew closer, continuously fired hostile questions at the council leaders, who tried answering them as calmly and confidently as they could. Felix didn't know why his council colleagues bothered themselves, for no sooner did one or other begin to answer a question, than they were interrupted by another question. He quietly skirted around the reporters, ensuring he avoided eye contact, and used one of the side entrances to get inside the offices. No wonder I couldn't park, Felix thought to himself, whilst walking upstairs.

He walked into the main council office, and stopped dead in his tracks. There was paperwork spread over every desk and all over the floor. The only phones which weren't ringing were those which already had somebody speaking on them, attempting, from what Felix could understand, to justify the council's decision to redevelop the market square. Everywhere he looked, young people tried to get the council's computers back online. He glanced over at one of his colleagues for an explanation.

"Our website's gone down due to the number of angry e-mails posted on it by the general public. Not only that. We've been receiving letters by the truckload, most telling us it's the council who should be demolished not the wool shop. You've received your first death threat by the way," his colleague added.

"What?" Felix said.

"We all have. It was a round-robin death threat. Everyone on the council got one. That's not the half of it. The Guinness Book Of Records have declared the wool shop the oldest trading wool shop in Britain, and the longest, uninterrupted family-run business. They've also declared the Bailey sisters the UK's longest-serving retailers." His colleague doodled on a notepad as he spoke. "English Heritage have kindly telephoned to inform us that it has been drawn to their attention that the wool shop may be considerably older than previously believed, so now they want to carry out investigations at the property to find out how old it really is. If only one brick turns out to be mediaeval, they'll be making a formal application for the wool shop to be listed. Ever wish you hadn't started something?" his colleague quipped, looking up from his doodle.

Felix opened his mouth to say something, then closed it again. He wasn't sure he had anything constructive to say.

"Bet that tour of the States of theirs will be splashed all over the front pages," his colleague said to him, pointing a pen in his direction. "Rub our noses in it, why don't they? You wouldn't have thought a schoolboy's project could've opened up such a Pandora's box would you?"

Felix, who had always known when to retreat, figured now was as good a time as any.

"I'm not sure I'm going to be much use here. I'm going to my golf club," he muttered, hurrying out of the door. He paused to look out of the window. The press were still gathered at the front of the building – he'd use the back door.

II

Felix spent the rest of the afternoon at his club. A golf tournament showing at the clubhouse helped put all thoughts of wool shops and cause célèbres firmly out of his mind, and by the end of it, with his mood uplifted somewhat, he drove home.

His mood darkened again the moment he found a car he didn't recognise parked in his drive. He reached his front door just as it swung open, and an unknown woman stepped through it. He couldn't help noticing that she wore a camera around her neck.

"Perfect timing," Mirabella said, also stepping through the front door. "This is my husband," she informed the woman. Without warning the camera was pointed at Felix and his photograph taken.

"Would you like one of the two of us together?" Mirabella asked her.

"Please," the woman replied.

Before Felix was able to ask what was going on, Mirabella threw her arm around him and their photograph was taken.

"Thanks once again, Rector," the still unknown woman said to Mirabella. With a wave of her hand she was inside her car and gone, without having addressed a single word to Felix.

"You'll never guess who that was?" Mirabella asked from indoors.

"If this has anything to do with that confounded wool shop, or those three old ladies, then I really don't want to know."

"Okay then," she said nonchalantly, disappearing down the hallway towards the kitchen.

Felix reluctantly followed her. "Okay, tell me," he said irritably, knowing he was going to have to find out sooner or later.

"She was a journalist from one of the Dailies. She telephoned the rectory earlier, wanting to speak to you, but when I explained I was part of the campaign to keep the shop open, she suddenly seemed more interested in me than you, and came straight round to interview me."

Felix couldn't believe his ears. It was as though he was suddenly living in the twilight zone. He'd already received his first death threat, and now his face was going to be plastered all over the newspapers. He was a sitting duck. He wouldn't be able to leave his own house. In stunned silence, he watched his wife busy herself in the kitchen, chatting casually. "They said us being on different sides, so to speak, gave the story an even more interesting twist. It's lucky you arrived when you did," she said.

"For whom?"

CHAPTER THIRTY
The Long Arm of the Law

From the minute she'd sat in her parked car outside the Sheffield home of Peter Wilson, Jane had known this was a case which would end with her going to a police station. Whilst she genuinely believed she owed her clients a duty to protect their privacy, she couldn't allow Peter Wilson to continue abusing the trust placed in him by the people around him, including his own children. She was only too aware that if the case came to court, she would have to look into the eyes, not only of his wives, but of his heartbroken children, knowing that she was the one who'd brought matters to the fore, and that without her interference the people in that courtroom could possibly have spent the whole of their lives happily unaware of the treachery of the man they all loved. This thought was not something which lay easily with her. However she was a sensible woman and a serious crime had been committed, which it was her duty to report, and report it she would.

Minutes later, she walked into the police station and over to the duty sergeant at the reception desk.

"I've come to report a crime," she said wearily. "The crime of bigamy. Just to make things clear – I'm reporting it, not confessing to it."

After providing the duty sergeant with her details, Jane waited in one of the station's interview rooms. With chairs more comfortable than one might expect of a police interview room, and a photograph of an Italian hillside town hanging on the wall, Jane assumed the room was reserved for interviews with the general public.

The two officers assigned to take her evidence joined her there, taking seats on the other side of the desk. The older, and more senior of the two officers, Inspector Boyd, asked if she had any objection to the interview being recorded. She said she hadn't, and with the digital recorder switched on, Jane started to impart everything she knew about Peter Wilson to the officers. Thinking it best she began at the beginning, she explained she was a private detective to whom Orla Wilson had written. Neither Inspector Boyd, nor his assistant P.C. McKenzie, made any comment. She then produced the letter she'd received in the post from Orla and told them of their first, and to date only, face-to-face meeting.

"I met her for the first time at her Sunday school, where she told me she wanted me to follow her husband. I found her explanation for his absences rather incredible at the time."

Jane told the police everything. She passed those photographs she had over to them and also provided them with the relevant addresses in London, Sheffield and Manchester, together with the telephone numbers of both Winifred Wilson and Orla Wilson. She finished by telling the officers of her last conversation with Orla, including Orla's claim that her husband was with her when Jane knew he'd been in Manchester.

"She probably made it up to stop you coming here," McKenzie said.

"Initially I thought so too, but she was so adamant, insisting she could prove it that I gave the matter more thought. That's when I realised we could both be correct in what we saw," she explained. "Three old ladies provided me with the explanation." She told the officers the story of the day the Bailey sisters' coal was stolen by an Arthur Carter when plenty of witnesses swore he was elsewhere at the time of the crime and their explanation for it. "I left Peter Wilson at the apartment block in Manchester," Jane said, "I don't know how long he remained there for. It was still only mid-morning when I left. If he'd only stayed for a short time, made his excuses and left – something he clearly has a knack for – he could easily have driven from there to the airport, left his car there, and caught a local flight home. It's only a thirty minute flight. Without luggage, he only needs to be there an hour before. A taxi home and a story about where his car was, and poor Orla would be none the wiser. I checked the airport timetable. If he got the timing right, he could do it, door to door, in a little under two hours. He could even return to Manchester later the same day, or more likely, early the next morning, maybe even with Orla still asleep, and resume his double life – keeping all the ladies in his life happy. I'm sure your investigations will confirm my theory."

"I'm sure you're right, Mrs Hetherington," Inspector Boyd said. "Looks like he won't be spending Christmas with any of his families!"

"Don't look much, does he?" P.C. McKenzie said, staring at the photograph of Peter Wilson.

"It's often the way," Inspector Boyd replied. "So you're a private detective then?" he asked Jane. She nodded. "This your first bigamist, is it?"

"It is, but then I haven't been a private detective for very long." Jane explained. "Not yours, I presume?"

"Na," he said with a shake of his head. "Beats me why they do it. Seems a lot of aggro and expense to me.

They usually confess immediately, bigamists, I find, when they know the game's well and truly up."

"Should he confess, I presume I will not have to give evidence in court?"

He shook his head. "Shouldn't have to."

"I do so hope not," Jane said. "I'd rather not have to see the look of hurt and disbelief on the faces of all those he's lied to."

"No, that's our job, unfortunately," Inspector Boyd said. "Breaking news like that to people's never easy. We get training, but it's always hard."

"I have to warn you that Orla Wilson is unlikely to believe you at first."

"My guess, Mrs H., is that she'll never believe it, even if and when he pleads guilty. We see a lot of that kind of thing in this job. Had a husband once whose wife tried to kill him by poisoning his curry. She even told us how she'd done it, and what she used, but he still didn't believe it. He still visits her in jail, telling everyone who'll listen that she's innocent. Too painful for him to accept the truth, poor bugger."

CHAPTER THIRTY-ONE
Fifteen Minutes of Infamy

Alone at last, Felix quietly completed the crossword at the kitchen table. He'd just put his pen down when Penny ran into the kitchen and began pulling at his arm. "You've got to come with me now, granddad," she said.

"Who says?"

"Grandma."

He reluctantly got to his feet. Penny took his hand and half-dragged him into the front room, where Miles sprawled on the floor, Susannah sat in an armchair and Mirabella lounged on the sofa. Penny ran across the room and climbed up on her mother's lap, as Mirabella pointed at the TV and shouted, "It's us, it's us. We're on breakfast TV."

To Felix's horror, one of the breakfast television presenters held open a morning newspaper, displaying the photograph of him with Mirabella taken on their doorstep the day before.

"This is an interesting story, Judy," the breakfast TV presenter said. "Mirabella Dawson-Jones and Felix Dawson-Jones are a married couple who live in Failsham, the small market town in Hoven which has found itself the centre of international attention."

"And maybe you could remind everybody, Ben, why this small town has found itself the subject of such speculation," his co-host asked him.

"As if we need to be reminded," Felix said miserably, slumping down next to his wife on the sofa.

Miles grinned at his sister and niece.

"Well, Judy," breakfast TV Ben said. "Failsham's market square is due to be modernised, which will mean that a very old wool shop, which we now know has been trading from there for centuries, will be knocked down. Furthermore, the three sisters, all in their eighties, who still run the wool shop…"

"… and who are now known to be Britain's oldest retailers," Judy said.

"Yes Judy," Ben said, "will be forced out of the home they have lived in for all of their lives."

Felix Dawson-Jones leapt to his feet and began pointing at the television.

"They will end their days in a beautiful new home," he roared. "I would like to live in their new home. Is this objective reporting? Is it?" Felix shouted helplessly at the television set.

"And how are Mr and Mrs Dawson-Jones involved in all of this?" Judy asked her co-presenter.

"Well, Judy," Ben began, "it's actually Mr Dawson-Jones and the Rev. Mrs Dawson-Jones because Mrs Dawson-Jones is in fact the local rector."

"A rector, being a caring person, would naturally want to help the three sisters keep their little shop open," Judy said.

"Naturally," Mirabella said, whilst her husband threw his hands up into the air and said, "Could this be any more one-sided?"

"Naturally," Ben also said. "The Rev. Dawson-Jones is in fact spearheading the campaign to keep the shop open."

"And a very successful campaign it's turning out to be," Judy said.

"It certainly is," her colleague agreed, adding, "however her husband is a member of the council who want to knock down the wool shop."

"Good heavens!" Judy feigned. "Boo! Hiss!"

"Boo! Hiss!" Penny mimicked.

Felix buried his head in his hands, whilst beside him, his wife beamed.

"Is this causing arguments in the Dawson-Jones household?" Judy asked.

"Yes," Felix Dawson-Jones said darkly, from the comfort of his living room sofa.

"No," Ben said brightly, from the comfort of the breakfast TV sofa. "Quite the contrary apparently. The Rev. Dawson-Jones has been quoted as saying that she and her husband have been happily married for over twenty years, and in such a length of time as that, even a couple as happy as them, can't be expected to agree on every issue."

"Well let's hope everything turns out for the best," Judy said. "Maybe we should invite Mr and the Rev. Dawson-Jones on the show?" she added.

Felix found himself poked in the ribs by his wife.

"Wouldn't that be nice?"

"I'd rather be boiled in a vat of oil," he replied.

"That photograph of you, Mum, is very flattering," Miles told her. "They've made you look younger and slimmer than you really are," he said cheekily. "That means the press like you when they do that."

"That'll be why they've made me look petulant and slightly deranged," Felix said, in despair.

CHAPTER THIRTY-TWO
Angela

Jane hadn't slept well. She knew reporting Peter Wilson to the police was not only the right thing to do, it was the only thing she could have done, this however, didn't make her feel any better. How typical, she thought to herself. There you are, a decent woman, beating yourself up over the actions of somebody else who will never appreciate or care about the pain and emotional carnage he's caused others.

The morning looked as though it would at least be sunny. Rather than sit around moping, she decided to start her dahlia tubers and with her gardening bag in hand, walked over to her greenhouse.

There, she filled a shallow plant tray with compost, laid the roots across it, sprayed them with water and placed the tray in direct sunlight. This didn't take nearly long enough. Neither did watering the sweet pea seeds she'd planted the month before, nor deadheading and watering her other greenhouse plants. Even after spending some time tidying up her greenhouse, she still felt uneasy about the events of the last few days. She wondered what else she could find to distract her. She knew what she'd do – she'd prune her Yew tree. Ordinarily that would be a job for her gardener, but extraordinary times called for extraordinary measures.

Donning thick gloves and a padded jacket to protect her against the brambles, she set about the task with the *Play for the Day* playing in the background on the radio. It was strenuous work, and the gloves and jacket just made her hotter than she would otherwise have been. Nonetheless, the time went quickly. The

Play for the Day ended with someone being pushed down the stairs by an unknown assailant. They should get a private detective in, Jane thought to herself, while on the radio, the programme's presenter said, "After the news, I'll be interviewing the president of the Jasper August society, John Stem. If you want to know who Jasper August is, and why he needs his own society, listen on."

Jane almost fell over. Good heavens, she said out loud. Now this she had to hear. She quickly made herself a cup of tea and took it with her to the conservatory, where – warmed through by the under-floor heating, the tea in her hands and her legs raised up on a footstool – she settled herself down, feeling far more relaxed than when she'd woken up.

On the radio, the presenter said, "You've come to tell us how sketches of a beautiful young woman called Angela, have resurfaced decades after they disappeared? Am I right?"

"You are."

"Please tell the listeners how the sketches were discovered and why their discovery completes a story?"

"I was at home one morning, pottering about, when I received a telephone call from a good friend of mine who happens to be the owner of an art gallery," John Stem said. "He was telephoning me with the most extraordinary news – an old lady had just walked off the street with none other than the missing Jasper August sketches of Angela, under her arm."

"Old lady," Jane repeated sarcastically, suddenly no longer so relaxed. "Old lady?"

She calmed herself down enough to be able to listen to the rest of the interview.

185

"I drove straight there," John Stem continued. "The minute I saw the sketches, I knew they are authentic."

"How?" the interviewer asked.

"For a number of reasons. We know from August himself that they existed. He'd described them in some detail, and the collection of sketches we'd been given, matched those details exactly. Besides, I'd know that unique technique of his anywhere. August could even use charcoal to portray personality. I knew in my gut they were by him, long before Fonebies authenticated them."

"Where have they been all this time?"

"The lady's husband acquired them somehow or other, many years earlier. Neither of them realized their true value. He has now died, and she decided to sell them. She chose the gallery she did at random, thankfully. Another gallery might not have realised what they were."

"Did you give the old lady a good price for it?" the interviewer teased.

"Not you too," Jane said tersely.

"I can assure you we paid her the full market value. She should be one very happy lady."

"Well she's not," Jane said.

"It must have been a wonderful moment, when you knew it was yours."

"It's a dream for all of us in this business, that one day something like that will happen, but that it happened to me. I can't express how I feel in words." He sounded almost as though he was too overcome to continue.

He wasn't the only one who was emotional. By now Jane, who had heard herself described as an old lady too many times, was fuming. Sixty-three-year-old Jane didn't think of herself as being old. She also found it intensely irritating to be described as old by someone clearly older than herself. Old lady, she muttered. Well, we'll see who lives the longest, John Stem, she thought to herself. Still angry, she picked up the secateurs again and began to violently prune a hybrid rose, which, until she started pruning it, had stood in the corner of the conservatory looking rather sorry for itself. When she'd finished, she was surrounded by rose cuttings. She always found gardening cathartic, and pruning the rose bush had done the trick. She was beginning to feel less annoyed. Her mood was further buoyed when the presenter announced a scoop. It wasn't only the whereabouts of the sketches of Angela which had now come to light, but so too the whereabouts of the real Angela – the flesh and blood woman once painted by Jasper August.

"She's in the studio, and we'll be talking with her after the weather forecast."

Wow, thought Jane. This was the woman she'd heard Graham Burslem describe as, 'half fire-breathing dragon, and half she-wolf.' Well, this should be entertaining, at least, she thought, rather hoping she was about to hear a woman even more prickly and difficult than Jane herself felt. She lay the secateurs on the rose cuttings, dropped her gardening gloves on top of both, and stretched out in her wicker chair. She wanted to be comfortable to hear to this.

"You must understand, I'd only just turned eighteen when I met Jasper," she heard Angela explain, minutes later. "We were young and so in love, at least I was, and I like to think that Jasper was too," she giggled. "I can't tell you how in love with that man I was. That's probably why I never married; no one has ever come close to him in my affections. He was the most charismatic and attractive man I've ever met, but then I had gone to a convent school, so I didn't have a great deal of experience to fall back on," she added. "That Jasper chose me for his muse was beyond my wildest dreams. I would have done anything for that man, anything. I probably still would."

Jane slowly turned her head to stare at the radio. Something about Angela's words made her feel very troubled indeed.

"For five years of my life, I supported his career completely," Angela continued. "I even dropped out of university. It was I who worked at all manner of things just to support him, so he could paint. He was consumed by his art and so was I. At one time, I was working as a secretary during the day and a waitress at night, and all Jasper was doing was painting, but I didn't mind. I believed he was a genius and still do.

"I knew he'd be successful one day and he was, but that success came at a price. Jasper was completely at ease with his growing celebrity, but I was not. I felt out of place at the type of events we began to get invited to. Everyone wanted to talk to him. No one was interested in me, quiet, mousey Angela. While Jasper circled the room, I'd spend most of the evening alone, nervously biting my nails, hoping I didn't make a fool of myself, if anyone did get around to speaking to me. All these events were the same. Jasper chatted easily, basking in the compliments he was paid, while I was ignored and overlooked. Needless to say, I started making excuses not to go and he stopped inviting me. I don't think he resented me not going, quite the opposite. I think he felt he deserved a more glamorous girlfriend. Certainly the girlfriends he had after me were very glamorous indeed. By the end, we were living different lives and it was time to go our separate ways. We split up when I was twenty-four and I wasn't to speak to him again," she said sadly.

Angela's words weren't spoken in bitterness, in fact, to Jane they came across as quite the opposite. Jane thought Angela was still besotted with Jasper August.

"I'm amazed to read about myself as being discovered. I really am. I can't believe that anybody is interested in me, a middle-aged spinster."

Jane didn't want to hear any more. She got up and turned the radio off. She stood motionless by the radio for some time, staring at it in a mixture of horror and disbelief, replaying Angela's words in her mind. Oh my God, she said to herself, as the truth dawned. Despite being on her guard, despite all the investigations she'd made, somehow she'd allowed herself to become a party to a con trick. She'd been taken in by the oldest trick in the book. How could she have been so gullible?

CHAPTER THIRTY-THREE
The Duties of a Public Servant

Felix didn't ordinarily suffer from paranoia, but he did not think he was imagining it when he felt people were pointing at him, or sniggering at him when he took his morning stroll into the town centre. Nor did he think he was imagining a slightly sarcastic tone to the words, "Morning Mr Dawson-Jones," used by the girl behind the counter of his favourite coffee bar, when he purchased his coffee and muffin.

Ordinarily he would have chosen a seat by the window, but today he decided to sit at a corner table, his head buried in a newspaper. The only comfort he could draw from all of this was the conversation he'd overheard between his wife and daughter, when he'd walked past the study and heard Mirabella exclaim, "What on earth are we going to do, Susannah? I didn't think we were going to get anything like as many orders for wool as this? How are we going to deal with all of this? We can't just ignore them. You'll have to go to the post office to buy envelopes and stamps."

"If orders keep coming in like this, we'll be doing this for the rest of the day and still be no further forward," he heard Susannah say. "I don't resent helping the Bailey sisters out, but if people keep ordering wool from them at this rate, they'll out-live us."

He'd tittered as he'd left the house. He tittered again when he remembered it, settling down to drink his coffee and read his paper. A little while later, Felix popped the last of the muffin into his mouth and drained his second coffee cup. He folded up his newspaper and strode out of the coffee shop to walk home.

Back at the rectory, didn't find his wife and daughter furiously packing wool as he'd expected. Instead, he found Mirabella waiting for him pensively.

"What's wrong?" he asked.

"I've just received a telephone call. The Bailey sisters have locked themselves in their wool shop and are refusing to leave it."

"What about New York? Isn't that today?"

"They don't want to go anymore."

CHAPTER THIRTY-FOUR
Blue Moon Art and Crafts

I

Jane literally ran to the phone and called Graham Burslem's mobile phone number. The number had been disconnected. She called his home number and left a message on his answer phone, asking he call her back straightaway. She also called the number she had for Lionel Scott, but it too was disconnected. Finally she called the Beech Hill Art Gallery. A young woman answered the phone and said, "Blue Moon Art and Crafts."

"I thought this was the number for the Beech Hill Art Gallery," Jane said.

"That's closed down."

Jane took a deep breath and continued, "I'm trying to get hold of a Graham Burslem. This is the only number I have for him. I wonder if you know him, or how I may get hold of him?"

"I'm sorry. I've never heard of him."

Jane closed her eyes and replaced the receiver without saying a word.

She arrived at the Blue Moon Art and Crafts shop, less than an hour later. The notice next to the door, proclaiming Lionel Scott the gallery's owner, had disappeared. Still short of breath, Jane opened the door and stepped inside. A young woman, presumably the young woman who answered the phone, sat behind the till. She smiled at Jane as she stepped into the shop. The shop sold ethnic jewellery and clothes, natural beauty products, trinkets, cards, scented candles and other miscellaneous items aimed at the young female market. The shop was devoid of customers.

"You wouldn't happen to know what happened to the man who ran the art gallery that was here before – the Beech Hill Art Gallery – would you?"

"Its owner wanted to retire and my dad bought the lease from him," the young woman said.

"When?"

"A few months back."

"But I was only at an exhibition at it a few weeks ago," Jane asked.

"That wasn't the same gallery."

"But it was called the Beech Hill Art Gallery."

"It may have been, but like I said, the Beech Hill Art Gallery's owners sold up months ago. After we put in for permission to change the building's use so I could open my shop, some man rang my dad up. He'd seen the notices about the change of use application and realising dad'd bought the gallery and was going to turn it into a shop, he asked if he could sublet the place for a couple of months while it was still technically an art gallery. He said he wanted to display his daughter's artwork to the world. She's a recent graduate from some art school apparently. She sounds a bit spoilt to me. Anyway my dad couldn't see the harm in it, so he said okay. Got him a bit of money. It must have been the girl's exhibition you went to. Anyway, they've gone and I am here." The girl swept her arms around in a wide flamboyant movement.

Tell me about it, Jane thought grimly.

"Did this man tell your dad his name and address, by any chance?" Jane asked, although, even as she asked the question, she didn't know why she'd bothered herself. She knew damn well that whatever name and address Graham Burslem had given to this girl's father, it would obviously be as false as everything he'd told her. The only genuine information Graham Burslem had given Jane, she knew, were his bank account details.

"I think it may have been Ken something. Ken Black maybe. I don't really know. I could find out from my dad if you want?" the girl said helpfully.

"No, that will not be necessary, dear," Jane said wearily.

She purchased some cards and a candle as a mark of her gratitude to the girl for her troubles. She paused by the door and said, "Is your father's name Lionel Scott, by any chance?"

"It is, yeah. Do know him?"

II

Except for the envelopes lying scattered on the gallery's floor, nothing in the gallery appeared to have altered since the last time Jane peered through its windows. The same pictures hung on its walls, the same newspaper clipping was displayed in its window, and the same notice declared the gallery closed for the winter. Even the oil painting Graham Burslem had given her as a thank you present was mysteriously back on the wall.

From the gallery, she drove to Graham Burslem's house. It didn't look as though anyone was at home. There weren't any cars parked in the drive. She knocked at the front door and waited, but no one answered it. She peered through the windows, but the house was in darkness. She called Graham Burslem's

194

home telephone number. She heard the telephone ringing inside the house, but her call was picked up by the answer phone. She didn't bother leaving another message.

She walked around to the back of the house and tried the back door, but it too was locked. She walked to the end of the garden and looked up, hoping to see movement inside, but saw none. The house looked as though it was deserted. She could only suppose 'Jenny Burslem' an accomplice to this elaborate con, along with 'Lionel Scott'.

An upper storey window of a neighbouring house opened and a woman appeared.

"Who are you?" the neighbour demanded. Her tone was sharp. "What are you doing in the Burslem's back garden?"

"I'm terribly sorry. I hope I didn't disturb you. I was trying to see if anyone was in. I've travelled some way to buy some art from the gallery, but it's closed," Jane said. "Does Graham Burslem live here? I thought he did, but there doesn't seem to be anyone here either. I'll slip a note through the letterbox, if this is the right address."

The neighbour visibly mellowed. "It's the right address alright," she said. "I'm sorry if I was a bit abrupt, but they had a break-in a while ago. They didn't get much – a couple of bottles of wine and some cash is all – but we've all been on our guard since."

"I'm sorry to hear that. Might you know when Graham is expected home? Is it worth my while waiting?"

The neighbour hesitated before answering. "I think your note would be a better idea. Graham's not a well man that he's not. I don't want to say too much, least I speak out of turn. You'd better speak to a member of the family. They'll be home soon, right enough. I expect they're visiting him in the hospital at the moment."

Jane forced herself to remain composed. "My goodness. I had no idea. Has he been unwell for very long?"

"Quite long enough, I'm afraid. Like I say, I don't want to say too much."

"Of course you don't. I quite understand. I think I'll leave it for the time being. I'm sorry to have disturbed you."

Jane was almost in a trance when she got back to her car. The man who sold her that sketches must have learnt, somehow or other, of Graham Burslem's illness and set about taking over his identity. For that he needed a passport and so he'd broken into the Burslem's home. He must have taken the wine and cash as a clever subterfuge. She had to admit it was ingenious. If only Mrs Burslem had looked more thoroughly when she'd discovered the break-in, she might have noticed a bill missing, as well as her husband's passport and one of his ties. But she hadn't, not with her husband seriously ill in hospital. Either the sketch-pad was stolen (how he'd come across the sketches and taken them without anybody noticing, was anyone's guess) or most likely, they were a set of forgeries on a pad once handled by Jasper August.

Jane closed her eyes. The passport and bill were more than enough for the imposter to open a bank account in Graham Burslem's name. The same bank account she'd just sent James Haley's money to. The phone rang. To her surprise she saw Graham Burslem's home number displayed. She answered it.

"Hello," she said hesitantly.

To her surprise, she heard Jenny Burslem's distinctive voice at the end of the line.

"I believe you left a message for Graham Burslem. I'm afraid Graham isn't very well at the moment. Is there anything I can help you with? I'm his sister-in-law, Jenny."

Did she say sister-in-law, Jane thought.

"I've just heard that poor Graham's been unwell," Jane said. "I'm an occasional customer to the gallery. I just wanted to speak to his wife to enquire after his health, and ask her to pass my best wishes on to her husband."

"Well, Graham isn't actually married," Jenny Burslem said, "but I can assure you the doctors are doing everything they can for him and we're here to look after him when he gets home. Can I tell him who's called?"

"No it's all right. I'll send a card," Jane said.

She threw her phone on to the passenger seat and pressed her forehead against the steering wheel.

'Even my wife, Jenny, doesn't know how bad things are,' he'd said. Nice touch 'Graham' she thought.

She couldn't worry about the why's and the wherefore's now. She must get hold of James Haley without delay. From her car, she telephoned the Diamond Gallery in London. Its answer phone stated the gallery closed, and asked the caller to leave their name, telephone number, and any message, if they wished their call to be returned.

"Mr Haley, this is Jane Hetherington. I'm the lady who sold you the sketches of Angela. Mr Haley, there is no easy way to tell you this, but I believe, despite the fact that other parties have authenticated them, that the sketches I sold you are stolen or forged. In fact I'm certain of it. I'm afraid we have both been duped by a very clever and cunning man. I think it would be best if we met. There isn't time for me to come down to London today, and therefore I will come to your gallery first thing tomorrow. If you get this message before then, please do call me."

CHAPTER THIRTY-FIVE
The Oldest Trick in the Book

Although it was already passed nine o'clock on a weekday morning when Jane arrived at the Diamond Art Gallery, the gallery still hadn't opened. She peered through the window but couldn't see anyone around. She knocked a few times on the front door. No one answered it. She tried it, but it was locked. She went to the empty rear car park, to try her luck at the back, but was just as unsuccessful. She looked up at the roof garden and saw a deck chair.

"Mr Haley, James," she called out, as loudly as she could. "It's Jane Hetherington. I need to talk to you.

From the car park, she saw him turn to look down. She wasn't certain whether or not he'd seen her. He didn't acknowledge her, but she watched him stand up and leave the roof garden. She stayed where she was. A few minutes later she heard the back door unlock, then nothing. She walked over to the door and tried it. This time it opened. She let herself in and found herself in the gallery's private quarters. This too, lay in darkness. There wasn't any sign of James Haley. Jane climbed up the stairs towards a closed door. At the top of the stairs, she pushed the door open and stepped outside onto the roof garden.

From his deckchair, James Haley stared at a tablet computer, propped up on the table. Jane pulled up a garden chair and sat down next to him. He nervously played with a postcard, turning it over and over in his hands. He seemed to be watching a film.

"I'm so sorry, James," Jane said. "Everything I did, I believed to be for the best. A man masquerading as a

199

local art dealer called Graham Burslem asked me to sell the sketches on his behalf, persuading me of his very good reasons for being unable sell them himself. Although I did not know it, the actual art dealer was, and still is, seriously ill in hospital. The man who duped us both, knew this somehow and used it to perpetrate a scam."

James listened patiently, as Jane explained her part in the deceit. "He made himself look like the real thing. He completely took over his identity. He was extremely clever. Really very convincing. He even broke into the poor man's home and stole his passport, and other bits, including some mail, to make me believe him. He must have taken the spare keys to his gallery. I met him there. He even pretended to disable the alarm. I can only presume he'd either found out the code somehow or other, or had already disabled the alarm before I got there. I think he even went as far as impersonating a postman. He must have had at least one accomplice because I met him in the course of my investigations and he bore false witness.

"The fraudster had an answer for everything, and no doubt if I had suspected anything, or if I, or anyone else, had realised he wasn't who he said he was, he would have immediately disappeared." James Haley said nothing. "I heard an interview with Angela, and as soon as I did, I realised that despite what Graham Burslem, or whatever his real name is, told me, he couldn't have met the subject of the sketches. The woman I heard speak on the radio bore no resemblance to the woman he'd described to me. I knew instantly he had never met Angela. That part of his story was one lie too many. If he hadn't met Angela, then he could not

200

have been one of Jasper August's flat mates, and the sketches therefore could not be authentic."

James Haley began to laugh ruefully. Jane didn't know what to say. James Haley picked up a notepad from the floor by his chair. He opened it at a sketch he'd drawn there.

"Is this the man who told you his name was Graham Burslem?" he asked. "I sketched it from memory."

She studied the picture. This wasn't the man she met, or was it? The man in the sketch had very little hair whereas 'her man' as she called him, had a mass of thick curly hair. Her man had a beard and a moustache, whereas this man was clean-shaven. The eyebrows were different, the nose of her man was more bulbous, and he was older, but then again, he had been disguised as another. The more she studied the picture, the more she realised it was the same man.

"Good Lord! You know him? Is this an insurance scam?" she demanded, ready to jump to her feet and go straight to the police.

"Oh that it were," he said. "I'm going to tell you something Jane. I've known this was a scam since I found this lying on my doormat," he said of the postcard he'd been fingering since she arrived at the gallery. "Now I'm going to tell you a story, which began many moons ago, and ended with this postcard being sent to me by the man who conned us."

She took it from him. The front of the postcard featured a painting of a Dutch couple from the nineteenth-century, walking hand-in-hand away from the artist, along a seashore on a blustery day, just as the sun was setting.

Jane turned the card over and read the message written on the back: 'Revenge is a dish best served cold!'

"Oh? It wasn't all about money, then?"

"It wasn't about money at all."

"I wouldn't mind a glass of that whisky you kindly offered me the last time I was here," she said.

James Haley returned with a bottle of whisky and two glasses. He poured both himself and Jane a measure. Jane sipped her drink.

"I'll admit to an errant youth," he began. "When I was a young man, the same age that Jasper August was when he painted Angela, I too was an artist, except that I was a counterfeiter. I'd done the artist struggling to choose between putting food in his belly or paint on his brush, just like Jasper August, only, unlike Jasper, I didn't have a doting girlfriend to support me, nor did I ever really have many original ideas, none which were very commercial anyway. I did however have a natural talent for copying works of art, which I quickly developed. To begin with, I painted things like Van Gogh's Sunflowers or Whistler's mother, things that couldn't possibly be authentic, and sold them from railway arches. No one who bought them could have possibly thought they were the real thing and the most I ever got for them was a tenner. You see, that's commerce. But where deception is involved, commerce turns into fraud. For an artist of my ability, there was more money in fraud than commerce. It didn't take me long to learn this, and to move from innocent reproduction into counterfeiting. I concentrated on the lesser-known artists, whose popularity was the reserve of the rarefied world of art connoisseurs. You wouldn't believe how many people fell for it.

"One day, about thirty years ago, I walked into a gallery, with one of my fakes concealed in a box. If you want to sell a counterfeit, you don't walk into a gallery with a dozen counterfeits, which, if they were authentic, would be worth millions. You walk into a gallery with one such piece, concealed in a box of rubbish. The type of tatty art that one old man could accumulate over a lifetime, say. Then you wait for someone to spot it, whilst desperately trying to pretend they haven't.

"This is where the man you know as Graham Burslem comes into it. His had been the third gallery I'd walked into that day, but none of the others had taken the bait. But he did. What our mutual friend thought he'd discovered, all those years ago, hidden in a pile of worthless tat, was the painting on this postcard." He waved the postcard in the air. "A Dutch landscape allegedly painted by an artist from the last century, called Leiff Uittenbogaard. Uittenbogaard's work was, and still is, in great demand. Of course it wasn't. It was a forgery of a picture catalogued as an Uittenbogaard but whose whereabouts was then unknown. I'd prepared a story. I pretended it, and the other paintings in the box, were my late uncle's art collection. I was charged with sorting out his estate and had no idea whether any of the paintings had any value, and maybe the owner of the gallery would be able to tell me? A story not unlike the one you told me, when you walked into my art gallery a few weeks ago," he pointed out. "The big difference being, whereas I gave you the true value of your painting had it been authentic, the man you know as Graham Burslem, was as greedy and dishonest as the man I was then. After looking through the paintings in the box, he told me that most of my uncle's art collection was frankly rubbish, but the Dutch painting was a nice picture. He explained that there was a certain amount of interest for such works from the discerning middle classes who liked pictures of that type for their dining rooms. He asked if I knew how my late uncle came to possess it. I said I thought my uncle had bought it from an unknown art gallery in Delft, while he was still a young man. As I spoke, I could tell from the look in his eyes that he knew the real value of what I was holding in my hands, or at least he thought he did. He offered me seven hundred pounds there and then, telling me he could sell it on for about one thousand pounds to some lady he knew was interested in that kind of thing. An original Leiff Uittenbogaard would have been worth the equivalent of seven thousand pounds to nine thousand pounds back then, you understand. He had to make me a half-way decent offer or I might have gone somewhere else, and he didn't want to lose it. I told him I might sell it at auction. He told me that was my choice, but that I might only sell the whole box for a couple of hundred or less, if it was a quiet day. Tell you what, he said, I'll give you a thousand for the five pictures in a box. Here and now, in cash, he said. Naturally I agreed. You drive a hard bargain, he said – the same words I used to you. He was true to his word and paid me a thousand pounds in cash, on the spot. I made a discreet exit. Not just from the shop, but from the area. I'd painted the whole lot for less than a fiver. I don't know how long it took him to find out, but when he did, it must have wiped that smug little look of his face."

"He went to all that trouble because you defrauded him a thousand pounds," Jane said.

"It was nearly thirty years ago," James said, "and a thousand pounds was a hell of a lot of money back then. I guess he's borne a grudge all that time, but he hasn't been able to find me before now."

"How did he? Did he chance upon you, or had he spent the last thirty years searching for you, do you think?" Jane asked.

"Probably a bit of both," James replied. "Almost a year ago, he walked in here, off the street. Whether he'd come across me online and come looking, or literally found me entirely by chance, I'll never know. I recognized him immediately. Being an artist, I never forget a face. He was so blasé the whole time he was here, that I didn't realise he'd also recognized me. But he had. He'd waited a long time to get his own back on me, and get back he did. Old August dying probably gave him the idea. He must have started hatching the plot the minute he walked out of here. I can only flatter myself that my fraud annoyed him so much that he went to so much trouble."

"Good God!" Jane said. "To have fooled so many he must be an even better forger than you were."

"The sketches aren't fakes, Jane. They're genuine. It was the man who sold them to me via you, who's the fake. Believe it or not, the original of this," James said, waving the postcard again, "was sold last week at auction in the far east. A white European man bought it. He paid cash." He picked up a tumble of whiskey and knocked it back in one, before slapping his thighs and reluctantly getting to his feet. "We'd better pay a visit to the police, I suppose."

"Yes, we must James," Jane said. "I think I'm also in possession of a forgery."

He shrugged and said, "the reason I gave up forgery was to spend more time with my family and less with the police."

The two walked over to the door.

"It's poor John Stem I feel sorry for," James Haley said, as the two walked down the stairs. "He's been dining out on his discovery, big time. He's even sent out invitations for an exhibit of the sketches." He laughed. "When this comes out, he'll be the art world's equivalent of the groom jilted at the altar!"

CHAPTER THIRTY- SIX

The Letter

I

Once home, Jane immediately checked her messages and found one from Mirabella.

"I don't know what's happened Jane," Mirabella said, after Jane returned her call. "I've called and called but they're not answering their phone. I even called their great-niece – the lady who was going to run the shop for them while they were away – but even she doesn't know why they've changed their mind. She just got a call from them late last night, telling her not to come down at all."

"How puzzling," Jane said. "I'll call on the wool shop now and see if they'll let me in."

II

But they didn't.

"We'd rather not speak to anyone at the moment if it's all the same to you Mrs Hetherington," Dotty Bailey said through the letterbox.

"I understand," Jane said, although she didn't. Just as she straightened herself up, she heard a voice in the background.

"Dotty – the letter!"

"Oh yes," Dotty said. "Would you mind posting a letter for us Mrs Hetherington?"

Jane bent down to the letterbox again and said that of course she didn't. "I think we've missed today's post," she added.

"Tomorrow will be more than adequate, thank you," Dotty said, passing a handwritten, stamped envelope through the letterbox to Jane.
She took it and and read the name and address on it, recognising the name. As there was nothing else she could do, she bid the ladies a good night, put the letter in her handbag and returned home to telephone Mirabella.

"What exactly happened when the Rolls-Royce turned up to take them to the airport?" she asked.

"Well," Mirabella replied, "it was very strange indeed."

III

After Jane came off the phone to Mirabella, she immediately telephoned the wool shop, but the Bailey sisters declined to answer. In that case there is only one thing for it, Jane said to herself, walking to her study and taking out some writing paper. She wrote a note to Lettice Bailey and slipped it into an envelope. She wrote Lettice's name on the front of the envelope and drove to the Market Square. After parking nearby, she pushed her note through the letterbox of the wool shop – then made her way to the cafe of a nearby supermarket. She was on her second coffee when her telephone rang. It was Nellie Bailey.

"Maybe you could call on us Mrs Hetherington?" she said.

"I'm on my way, Nellie dear," she said.

IV

The Nellie Bailey who answered the door was the most sombre Jane had ever seen her. Without saying a word, Jane embraced her and followed her into the shop. As they made their way through the shop and into the building's living quarters, Jane couldn't help noticing mail sacks leaning against the walls. "They're from well-wishers," Nellie said, matter-of-factly. "People are so kind. My sisters are waiting for you in the parlour," she added. Jane could see she was close to tears.

When Jane reached the parlour, Lettice and Dotty stood to greet her, both as sombre as their sister. Dotty motioned with her arm towards one of the chairs. "Please do take a seat, Mrs Hetherington."

The three sisters sat down on the Chesterfield, with Lettice in the middle. It was she who leant forward – Jane's letter in her hand. This she lay down on a small table, its contents exposed to everyone in the room.

My dear Lettice,

Please forgive my impertinence in writing to you. If anything I suggest in my note is untrue, or in any way offends you, then please accept my heartfelt apologies. I know you told the Reverend that your decision not to travel to America and appear on television there was because the publicity was all becoming too much for you. This we all understand. However, I do remember you saying how much you were enjoying the experience.

What I write next is merely a suggestion and yours to contradict or ignore completely, I will never raise it again.

Might the real reason for your change of heart be something else? Might it be your sudden realisation that with worldwide fame comes scrutiny? Maybe your real fear is of someone prying into your past and coming across something which happened many years ago? If I'm correct, and I think I might be, I can't believe anyone will think the less of you, because of something which happened when you must have been a very young woman – not after all this time.

If what I suggest is true, please let me help you, if I can.

Jane Hetherington

PS: I shall be in the town centre for the rest of the afternoon should you wish to call me on my mobile phone. Its number is...

"What makes you think this?" Lettice asked.

"You felt the urgent need to write a letter to your great neice, after suddenly cancelling your all-expenses-paid holiday to the United States, which I know you were looking forward to. I thought..." Jane stop talking. She could feel myself blushing – an unusual sensation for her.

"That our great-neice Andrea, is actually my granddaughter, the child of my illegitimate child, who I gave up to be raised by my brother, and the letter we asked you to post, was some type of confessional to her and her mother?" Lettice smiled gently when she said this. Jane realised immediately from the tone that she was mistaken. "Andrea is our brother's granddaughter, his daughter's daughter, nothing more," Lettice said.

"I'm so sorry Lettice. Since I've become a private detective my imagination sometimes runs away with me. I'll show myself out," Jane said, hurriedly getting to her feet.

"You will do no such thing Jane," Nellie said.

"We were ridiculous to think we could take such a secret to our graves," Dotty said.

210

In the wool shop's kitchen, Lettice calmly unlocked the cellar door and turned the overhead light on. She turned to Jane and said, "Come, please."

Jane followed Lettice through the open door, with Dotty and Nellie taking up the rear.

They made their way down the steep steps in single file. The cellar was brighter and less musty than Jane had imagined it would be. At the bottom of the stairs, Dotty and Lettice stood on either side Jane, while Nellie removed a small partition made from a curtain draped over some kind of frame, to reveal a small vase of fresh flowers. Something was written on the paving slab underneath it, but Jane couldn't make it out. She moved closer.

Harry Foraker - who lived for not a minute on earth but who will live in Heaven for ever

"We had to wait for Papa to die, before we were able to give him a gravestone," Lettice said.

Jane looked down on the grave of the child and, to her surprise, began to cry. She embraced Lettice with the words, "Oh Lettice. Your poor baby died."

Lettice gently shook her head. "Harry wasn't my baby, Jane."

Dotty lay her hand on Jane's shoulder. "Please don't cry Jane. My grief has deadened with time." To Jane's rather puzzled look, she said, "Lettice wasn't the only one of us with a boyfriend." She motioned towards the grave. "I named my son after his father Harry Foraker."

"Harry was my fiancé's elder brother," Lettice said.

"I genuinely loved Harry," Dotty explained. "He'd separated from his wife, but in those days divorce was a rich man's privilege. I only spend one night with him. He was going to war and I thought I might never see him again, which I didn't. I discovered I was pregnant after his death. I was unmarried teenager carrying a married man's child, which sixty-eight years ago Jane, wasn't an enviable situation to be in."

"Who else knew?" Jane asked.

"Outside this room, nobody," Dotty said. "Our mother was dying of cancer at the time. Our father spent most of the time with her at the hospital, or trying to keep his business running. When I became larger, I concealed my pregnancy through layers of clothing and kept out of Papa's way."

"A few times he even asked if Dotty was avoiding him, and we just told him not to be so silly," Nellie said.

"Our brother was only twelve years of age and away at school most of the time. He passed away last year, none the wiser," Lettice said.

"As I approached full-term, I simply didn't step outside. Nor did I help in the shop. Few could tell us apart even then, so I doubt anybody even noticed. The most painful thing was being unable to visit my mother in the hospital." She stopped to compose herself. "When my time came, I gave birth down here, to mask the noise, while Nellie and Lettice ran the shop."

"It wasn't just Dotty we had to protect Jane," Lettice explained. "There was Harry's widow and his children to consider."

"And Mama and Papa," Dotty said.

"You were alone?" Jane asked, horrified.

212

"For most of it, yes. Nellie was there for the end. At least we thought it was the end."

"We hadn't made any plans about what to do when the baby came," Nellie said. "I decided there and then to leave it on the church steps. I smuggled the baby out of the house wrapped in a blanket.I was in a blind panic. Luckily it was dark. I'd nearly reached the church, when a voice called out to me, 'Nellie Bailey – is that you – out at this time of night?' My heart nearly stopped. I spun around and saw Lady Jocelyn."

"Lady Amelia's mother," Lettice explained.

Nellie continued with her story. "She was taking one of her night strolls, accompanied by her maid. She hastened me over. I tried to conceal the newborn in my arms but she saw immediately what I held. She stared at the tiny bundle in my arms. 'Why this child is barely a few hours old,' she said. 'How have you come by a newborn?' In my terror, I did no more than blindly shake my head as though I didn't know. 'Is it a girl or boy?' she asked. 'Girl,' I managed to reply. 'She can't be yours. One of your sisters?' Lady Jocelyn asked. Again I shook my head, I remember the tears streaming down my face. 'What on earth are you intending to do with her?' she asked me. I remember my reply to this day. 'Oh ma'am, I have no idea.' She and her maid looked at each other. 'Give her to me,' she said. I hesitated. 'Hurry up girl or you'll be seen.' I did as I was bid. Lady Jocelyn took the baby and handed it to her maid who wrapped her under her cloak. 'We'll look after her tonight and tomorrow I'll visit my solicitor. He'll find her a good home.' As she spoke, her maid slipped away with the baby. 'It's for the best, Nellie,'

Lady Jocelyn said and I knew that it was. 'This will be our secret. We'll say no more about this.'

"When I returned home, Dotty was cradling Harry in her arms."

"I'd fallen pregnant with twins," Dotty said. "Just my luck! I wasn't as lucky with the second one as with the first, and little Harry was born dead."

"I was serving in the shop the whole time," Lettice said. "We had to keep up appearances."

Jane closed her eyes at the thought of it. She'd given birth in a hospital and even then it had nearly been a disaster. For the girl of just nineteen to give birth in a cellar, the second time alone – it was almost mediaeval! She put her hands on Dotty shoulders and held her close. "Dotty, you poor dear thing. All those years. Watching me with Adele. It must have been agony for you."

"The decades had passed, even then Jane," Dotty said. "I recovered quickly. I was only nineteen. Mama eventually passed away. Papa lived for many years afterwards, although he was never really the same again. We carried on with our lives. Neither Papa nor our brother, ever knew what happened."

"And you don't know what happened to her after that?" Jane asked.

"A year later, Lady Jocelyn called at the shop with her maid on the pretext of buying wool," Lettice said. "She asked if we were alone in the house and when we said we were, she produced a lock of hair and a photograph of the baby. She told us her new family had called her Rose and promised Rose lacked for nothing. Other than this we know nothing about what became of her. We don't even know if she is aware she's adopted."

"I think I need a cup of tea," Jane said.

Upstairs in the kitchen, Lettice pressed a mug of tea into Jane's hands, while Dotty laid a photograph out on the kitchen table. Jane picked it up. It was a black-and-white photograph of a smiling child of about one year of age, a ribbon tied around her head. Jane put the photograph down. So, Hugh had been right all along. The sisters had been nursing a secret, a secret they'd had to cut themselves off from the world to keep and, as a result, had come to be seen as increasingly eccentric, something they didn't play down. Just one of the many prices they'd paid.

"You were wrong about one thing Jane," Lettice said. "It wasn't the publicity we feared, for there are few alive who even know what happened that night."

"What caused us to panic and threw up the drawbridge was the call we received from English Heritage," Dotty said.

"They asked if they could begin their survey of the wool shop when we were away," Nellie said. "I asked what they meant by survey and they said nothing much more than walking around the place, although they might need to dig outside or in the cellar."

"We realised then that we couldn't keep our secret hidden any longer. If English Heritage can't inspect our property as they wish to, it won't be listed and the council will demolish it," Lettice said. "After reflection we decided to write to Andrea setting out the bare facts of the matter. Sometimes it's easier to put these things in writing."

215

"I also realised something," Dotty said. "Not only can't I keep my secret any longer, I don't want to. If she can be found, Rose has a right to know her providence and that she had a big brother. Her father's other children also have a right to learn about her; and my son deserves a Christian burial."

CHAPTER THIRTY- SEVEN

Read All About It

The following Sunday, Jane received a text from James
Haley: 'Read today's Sunday Era!'

She'd need to go into town to buy one she realised,
and so, at just before nine in the morning, Jane closed
the door of her cottage behind her. With the sky grey
and a thick, morning mist still shrouding the stand of
trees at the neighbouring field's far end, it was hard to
tell where the land ended and the sky began. She
walked along Cuckoo Tree Lane towards town. The
crisp frost had petrified the spider's webs in the rosehip
bush, iced its blood red berries, and turned the crops in
the field white. It also made the ground slippery and
more than once Jane nearly slipped on the icy path.

In the market square, she bought a copy of the
newspaper and took it with her to a nearby coffee shop
to read. On the supplement's front page was a
photograph of James Haley, pictured outside his
London art gallery, under the words: '*It takes a thief to
catch out a thief!*'

The caption invited readers to read an interview
with (as the magazine put it) 'A swindled swindler.'

The article was written in the first person,
confessional style and began with James Haley boasting
about his early successes as an art forger, including a
very detailed account of his deception of 'Graham
Burslem', whom he referred to throughout as Jim
Grady. 'I couldn't visit the southwest coast for a very
long time after that!' he quipped. 'I was one of the very

217

best, if I say so myself,' he told the readers, warning them never to underestimate the number of forgeries there were out there. He bragged about his long career and how he had pulled the wool over the eyes of many an art critic, art gallery, museum and private collector. 'Now, I can't name names or anything, but there is one very rich and famous rock musician, whose art collection isn't quite as valuable as he thinks it is!'

James Haley recalled his time in jail. 'They were mostly open jails, so it wasn't a big deal. When I got married and had a kid, I didn't want my boy to have a jailbird as a dad, so I packed it in and went legit. I became quite a successful art dealer. I knew who to trust,' he declared, before dramatically informing the readers that, although he didn't know it: 'There was one crime, I still hadn't done my time for. I'd made an enemy, and one with a long memory at that. My past was about to catch up with me big time. The fates were to throw me and him together and that was that. I always thought I'd be able to tell a fake from a real 'un. But it turned out, I couldn't!'

He added that although police investigations were underway, he personally doubted he would ever see his money again, or anyone jailed for the crime.

The interview ended humbly. 'If you're reading this, old fruit, then hats off to you, mate, you've pulled off your coup brilliantly. Let's just call it quits, eh?'

Jane laughed out loud at James Haley's cocky honesty and self-effacement. She couldn't help but admire his attitude. He accepted he'd been duped with good humour, and rather than vowing to avenge it, he'd put the whole thing down to experience, unlike his foe. The world, she decided, needed more people like James

Haley in it. The older, wiser James Haley, not the young forger, obviously.

James Haley's sketch of 'Graham Burslem' appeared at the bottom of the article alongside the name and number of the police officer in charge of the investigation, for any who had more information. Jane ripped the article out of the magazine, and put it in her handbag. The next time she felt low, she'd take the article out and reread it.

CHAPTER THIRTY-EIGHT

Closure

I

Felix met the coroner emerging from the cellar. As soon as he saw Felix sitting at the kitchen table, the coroner scowled and snapped, "The police shouldn't have let you in here. What are you doing here?"

"I'm a family friend of old," Felix explained. "My wife is the local rector. The Bailey sisters are with her at the moment at the rectory. Here, let me show you some ID."

The coroner glanced at a young police officer guarding the back door. He nodded to confirm Felix's story. The coroner mellowed. Before Felix could ask if there was any news, the coroner said, "We haven't found more than a fragment of thighbone. There isn't enough here even to sex the child, let alone say whether he was born dead or alive. Realistically the most any of them could be charged with is preventing the lawful burial of a body. Ultimately it's up to CPS, but I would have thought that at their age the charge will be allowed to lie on the file."

Felix thanked the coroner and called his wife.

II

On a cold, damp morning, a small funeral party, consisting of three elderly sisters, the rector, her husband and a friend, left a churchyard for a rectory.

From the road a local reporter shouted out, "How do you feel Ms Bailey?"

Dotty ignored Felix's entreaty not to say anything and walked over to speak to him. "A burden has been lifted from my shoulders. My child has been given a

220

Christian burial and I remain hopeful of seeing my daughter again before I die, so how do you think I feel, young man?"

"At least he had the decency to look shamefaced," Felix said, as they reached the rectory.

At the door, Susannah took their coats. "I've left some tea and some sandwiches in the drawing-room," she said, "and lit a fire."

III

The party made themselves comfortable in the warm drawing-room. As always, the three sisters sat beside each other along a sofa. Felix poured their tea and Mirabella placed a selection of sandwiches onto side plates, which Jane handed out.

"We finally found a bungalow," Lettice announced, taking a plate of sandwiches. "We didn't think we'd ever find anything we all liked. We're all so different, you see, aren't we, girls?"

"But then we saw a lovely bungalow, and we all liked it immediately," Nellie said. "It has three bedrooms and is just the right size for us."

"It's so modern. Ovens and fridges at waist-height. Everything on one floor," Lettice said. "It even has a freezer – we've never had one before."

"It will be so much easier to heat than the wool shop, I imagine," Jane said.

"It will, and it's near the city centre," Dotty said.

"It's on a bus route and has shops nearby," Lettice said.

"And a doctor's surgery," Dotty said.

"And a park with a duck pond," Nellie said.

"Well that is good news," Felix said.

"Won't you miss the wool shop?" Jane asked.

"We love our home, Jane," Dotty explained. "It holds so many memories, but it's getting harder and harder to live there. It takes two of us to turn on a tap. Walking up and down stairs at our age takes so long, that by the time we get downstairs in the morning, it's almost time to go upstairs again."

"It's time to move on," Lettice said.

The party fell silent and Felix hurriedly refilled everybody's teacups.

As she picked up her teacup, Lettice's eyes fell on something on a nearby table. Jane knew what she was looking at – it was a copy of the newspaper interview with James Haley, which Jane had earlier given Felix and Mirabella. "What's this?" Lettice asked, picking up the article to read.

"My claim to fame, I'm afraid," Jane said, rolling her eyes.

"Why this is Gary Carter," Lettice said.

On either side of her, her sisters studied the clipping.

"You know him?" Jane asked.

"We most certainly do," Nellie said. "For this is the son of Arthur Carter and Lady Amelia."

"The man who tried to steal from you?" Mirabella asked.

"As did his son," Dotty said, waving the clipping and adding dryly, "Like father, like son."

"This fellow," Felix said, pointing to the newspaper clipping, "also tried to steal your coal?"

Nellie took up the story. "Not coal, no. Common thievery wasn't good enough for Lady Amelia's son. He was a confidence trickster."

"He came to the wool shop pretending to be a man of God – a Salvationist who had taken the pledge. It was meant to make us trust him, and sell him something for less than we knew it was worth. He went as far as telling us his name was Eton Stewart," Lettice said. "What kind of name is that?"

"He sat in our parlour, telling us his name was Eton Stewart when we knew it wasn't, and our vase was only worth so much, we knew it was worth more," Dotty said.

"We knew him to be Gary Carter," Nellie said. "Disguise or no disguise, he still looked every bit his mother's son, but we knew him to be every bit as big as rogue as his father. It was Lettice who put him straight."

Lettice confirmed the story. "I certainly did. I said to him: 'Why are you telling us your name is Eton Stewart when we know full well you are Gary Carter, the son of that notorious villain Arthur Carter. We used to see you, and the poor woman who raised you, visiting your father in jail when we were visiting other more worthy prisoners.'"

Nellie carried on the story. "And once Lettice had said her piece, it was my turn. 'You don't fool us, mister,' I said."

"My goodness," Mirabella said. "Whatever did he do?"

"He left the area that very day," Lettice said.

"But like bad pennies always do, up he's turned again," Dotty said.

"I would appreciate it greatly if you could tell me all you know," Jane said.

"Are you helping the police investigate this case, Mrs Hetherington?" asked Nellie.

"I was an inadvertent party to this fraud," Jane explained. "The fraud was very elaborate and must have taken some time to plan. The fraudster was entirely convincing. He assumed the identity of another – an art dealer from Sailles. I don't think I should tell you his name, although he wasn't a party to the fraud."

The sisters looked at each other. It was Lettice who said, "Was it Graham Burslem, by any chance?"

"How on earth did you know?" Jane said.

"Well, Gary Carter does have more than a passing resemblance to Graham Burslem," Dotty said.

"You know Graham Burslem?" Jane asked.

"Oh yes – Nellie used to exhibit at his gallery. We've known Graham Burslem for many years," Dotty said.

"It's not surprising the two men look alike, in the circumstances," Nellie said.

"What circumstances?" Mirabella said, now on the edge of her seat.

"Graham Burslem is the son of Lady Amelia's sister," Lettice said.

"No!" Mirabella said.

The three sisters nodded.

"Poor Graham's been in hospital for some months now. He's had a stroke," Dotty said.

"His brother George, and his sister-in-law, Jenny, have had to move down to look after him, although George has now had to go back home because his elderly father's been taken ill," Nellie said.

"They don't want too many people knowing how ill he is. They might have to sell the gallery, they don't know yet," Lettice said. "It doesn't look as though he is going to get better."

"No?" Mirabella asked.

The three sisters shook their heads.

"He's suffered a relapse," Dotty said. "It's all so sad. It was the stress of his dear wife dying which caused all of this."

"They'd been together for more than thirty years, so sad," Nellie said.

"How do you think he got ahold of the original sketches?" Felix asked.

"He must have stolen them from Graham," Lettice said. "Graham is a very private man. After his wife died, he became even more solitary. Gary Carter must have contacted him. The two are cousins after all. He took advantage of his loneliness. He must have snooped around and come across them. A safe or a lock wouldn't stop him."

"But how did Graham Burslem have them?" Felix asked.

"Because he was once Jasper August's flatmate," Nellie said.

"So the story he told me was almost true, only he'd heard it from Graham Burslem?" Jane said.

"I bet the bugger meant to hang onto the sketches until old Burslem died, then flog 'em," Felix said, "only Burslem got ill, by which stage Carter had tracked down Hayley. Two birds – one stone!"

"What a thing to do – to take advantage of someone else's misfortune like that," Mirabella said. "Gary Carter is obviously a very clever man and an amoral opportunist. I don't think there was anything you could have done Jane. How could you have known?"

The sisters looked each other.

"There was a way you could have told Gary Carter and Graham Burslem apart, you know," Nellie said.

"Which is?" Jane asked wearily.

"Gary Carter is six foot one, but Graham Burslem is only five foot six!" Dotty said.

III

When Mirabella and Jane finally left the wool shop, it was early evening. They walked back along Common Lane together.

"It may not have turned out quite as we expected it to, Jane," Mirabella said, "but we promised the sisters we would help them and we have."

"And they've in turn helped me."

"Are you going to go to the police with your information about Gary Carter?"

"First thing, tomorrow morning."

"They'll be giving you your own chair soon," Mirabella teased.

They'd reached the fork in Common Lane which turned left into Cuckoo Tree Lane, and right into Rectory Lane, where they'd part company. As the two ladies said goodbye, a motorcyclist, swathed in leather and hidden by a helmet, roared past, tilting so much to one side that Jane wondered how he managed not to end up bumping along the road. Although the motorcyclist raised a hand in greeting as he sped by, neither recognized him.

"I wonder if he's one of Miles' friends?" Mirabella asked.

"Or Susannah?" Jane said.

"Don't even go there, her father and I can't go through that again," Mirabella said with a shudder.

CHAPTER THIRTY-NINE

Pandora's Box

I

It being the last day of the month, Jane opened the database on which she recorded a summary and the outcome of each case, and read through it, as was her custom at month's end. Roz's words came to mind,

"I didn't realise running for the local council would open up such a Pandora's Box."

The same could surely be said of Failsham Council's decision to try and redevelop the ageing market square; her own fateful decision to help 'Graham Burslem' sell his sketches; Orla Wilson's decision to instruct Jane to follow her husband; and who knows, possibly even Gary Carter's decision to try and defraud the Bailey sisters decades earlier.

She typed – Month Two: February – A Pandora's box!

Someone was knocking on her back door. She got up to answer it and found Jack grinning from ear to ear, clearly very excited about something. She was surprised to see him up at this time, it was still only mid-morning, and the teenager was not prone to getting up before the afternoon on weekends.

"You're up early?" Jane said, inviting him in.

"I had to come straight round with the news," he said, sounding so excited he almost couldn't talk.

"Has Charity won the lottery?"

"Almost as stupendous. Johnny's back!"

"Really?"

Now this was news. News she had to sit down to hear. "What happened to the Falkland Islands? He's hardly had time to get there and back?" she asked.

"Said it was too cold, but really, it's 'cos he missed me and Charity. He said so, when we were alone, me and 'im. He turned up on a motorcycle last night, with some lemons to make Pimms."

Typical Johnny, thought Jane. Pimms! In February!

"He said he saw you on the lane with Mirabella."

"Ah – so that's who it was!" she said.

"I was still at my friend's house when he arrived. Charity was one foot out of the front door. Any later and he'd've missed her. Not that it made any difference. She was so angry with him for just turning up out of the blue like that, she still went out. He had to spend the whole night in the house by himself. I got back this morning and found him still waiting. Charity's only now got back."

Would Charity take Johnny back, Jane wondered, and would he stay if she did?

"Is she going to take him back?"

Jack shrugged. "Dunno. That's why I'm here – give them some space."

"What do you think about it? I know what good friends you are."

"I like it when he's there, more than when he's not there. It's more fun when there's the three of us. It's good to have a man about the place. Charity does her best, but it's nice to have a bloke to talk to. But I hate it when he ups and leaves. It really upsets Charity, and it really upsets me. I told him as much. He said he came back because he loves us, and really missed us to bits, and if Charity takes him back, he won't ever leave again. I said, if he did, I'd hunt him down like a dog, and kill him and you'd help me. Hunting him down, I mean. Not killing him. I wouldn't expect you to do that, Jane. I'd do that myself!"

"Well we'd better hope that if Charity takes him back, he stays put, then hadn't we? I wouldn't want to be visiting you in jail for the next twenty years."

"I think he will," Jack said.

Jane got to her feet. She hoped Jack would be proved right. All Jane wanted for Charity and Jack was that they be happy; and she'd always had a soft spot for Johnny.

"I bought some of those toasted chocolate sandwiches the other day that you like so much," Jane said. "Would you like one for your breakfast?"

Jack said he would. "My day's getting better and better," he said, as Jane removed a couple of the frozen sandwiches from the freezer, and dropped them in the toaster. "All I need now is for Southstoft City to win Three - Nil!" he said.

II

Jane learnt later that Southstoft City went on to lose their match Three – Nil. She could only smile to herself when she heard that. Oh well, she thought. Two out of three
wasn't a bad result.

Also from Nina Jon:

Jane Hetherington's Adventures in Detection:

The Night of Harrison Monk's Death (1)

A Game of Cat and Mouse (3)

April (4)

www.ninajonbooks.com

A GAME OF CAT AND MOUSE
Jane Hetherington's Adventures in Detection: 3

CHAPTER ONE
Sisters! Sisters!

In kitchen of her sister's house, eighteen-year-old Lucy Erpingham poured two glasses of white wine and carried them over to the table where her sister, Jodie Narbade, peeled cellophane away from a selection of dips.

"Jodie, would you say you're very much the older sister?" Lucy asked, slumping down in the chair next to Jodie.

"What makes you ask?" Jodie replied.

"Some new guy has started at work and I got talking to him and said you were six years older than me. He said with an age gap like that, he bet you'd always been very much the older sister – that's what he said – and I said, what you mean bossy?"

Jodie helped herself to a breadstick. She knew what her sister really wanted to talk about. "Do you like him – this new guy?"

"A bit."

"A bit, eh? How old is he?"

"Bit older than me."

"Has he got a girlfriend?"

Instead of replying, Lucy opened a bag of crisps, dunked one of them in some of the dip and popped it in her mouth.

"What's his name?" Jodie asked.

With a mouthful of food, Lucy mumbled something incomprehensible, to which Jodie raised her wineglass and said, "Here's to Lucy and Mmunamable!"

"Me and Mmunamable! I wish we could do this more often, Jodie. Get together like this."

"I'm always here for you Lucy, you know that, but I'm a married woman now, I'm not at your beck and call anymore, love."

"Yeah, but I need someone to confide in."

"Why? What have you done?" Jodie teased. "Is that the door?" she asked just as the front doorbell rang for the second time. "Who on earth can that be at this time?"

She answered the door to find her neighbour looking quite flustered.

"I'm so glad you're in Jodie," he said. "My battery's flat and I'm already late. I need somebody to jump it. Is your husband about?"

"No, he's at a stag night, but don't worry I've got leads in the back of my car. I'll just get my keys."

She picked up her keys from the hall table, and called out to her sister, "Lucy I'm just helping my neighbour jump-start his car. I won't be long."

"Okay," Lucy called back.

II

Less than fifteen minutes later, Jodie walked back into the kitchen with the words, "Got him started." Lucy wasn't there. "Lucy? Where are you?" she called out.

Nobody replied, and so she knocked on the door of the downstairs cloakroom, but the door swung open,

233

revealing an empty room. Lucy wasn't in the living room either. Jodie yelled upstairs: "Lucy? Are you up there?"

When she didn't hear anything, she ran up the stairs but her sister wasn't anywhere that she could see. She returned to the kitchen. It was a bit like the *Marie Celeste* – the wine bottle was where she'd left it, as were their snacks and wineglasses, both still two thirds full. Where on earth was she? She was about to say, "I think you're a bit old for hide and seek, love," when she realised Lucy's handbag and coat were gone.

She called Lucy's mobile phone, but got the answer phone. "You gone home Lucy? Aren't you feeling very well?" she said. "At least call me and let me know you're okay." She sent the same message by text and received a reply by return.

'Had to go! Sorry. Things to do. C U!'

Jodie stared at the message. She'd never known her sister to do such a thing. It was completely out of character.

'What's happened? I'm here for you whatever you've done. But I can't help you if you won't tell me!' she immediately texted back.

She didn't get a reply and her calls went unanswered.

Made in the USA
Charleston, SC
20 November 2012